"You are cha[r]... in the county of Livingston, ...g the crime of..." The officer's voice trailed off as he gawked at the remaining words on the page. The single piece of paper he'd been holding escaped from his fingers as if on fire, and the yellowish sheaf fluttered to the wooden floor. At length, it came to rest in front of the defendant. "...Mayhem," he said after a long pause. His voice hissed out no louder than a mouse's squeak.

Her knees quaked while her head felt close to exploding. The hat she wore—made of whirls of fabric and ribbon piled close to a foot high—weighed upon her head as heavy as an anvil. She raised a trembling hand to swipe her brow as sweat bubbled on her skin. She blinked toward her attorney, but he continued to stare ahead, mimicking a statue in a park as he sat halfway twisted toward the judge and the jury. Sparkling pinpricks of light surrounded him like a ghost. She shook her head in hopes of clearing her sight.

She Wore
a Hat in Prison

by

Marion L. Cornett

Chapter One

Autumn of 1907

The judge's gavel marked the beginning of Zerelda's end. The *thwack* of the gavel hitting the block of wood hammered home the brutal reality of her being sent to prison.

"Zerelda Lena Boronza." An officer's voice, ominous and dark, came from the shadowy corner off to the judge's left, echoing throughout the dim-lit courtroom as eerie as a haunting specter. "Stand and hear the charge."

Zerelda looked to her right hoping her attorney held a magical power to still the shaking in her knees. Maybe offer up a look of reassurance or at the very least, a slight smile. Nothing. He stared straight ahead as if the knots in the wood-paneled walls a few feet away might swirl out smoke signals full of answers or solutions.

She had no choice but to stand. The captain's chair—hard wooden seat with spindles digging into her hips and spine with low wrap-around arms chafing her shoulder blades—was shoved so close to the long rectangular table she already felt imprisoned. Leveling her palms on the edge of the table, she pushed back. The spindly legs scraped on the wooden floor. The sound barked throughout the high-ceilinged room. She cringed and stood up.

"You are charged, by the great state of Michigan, in the county of Livingston, village of Cedartown, with the crime of..." The officer's voice trailed off as he gawked at the remaining words on the page. The single piece of paper he'd been holding escaped from his fingers as if on fire, and the yellowish sheaf fluttered to the wooden floor. At length, it came to rest in front of the defendant. "...Mayhem," he said after a long pause. His voice hissed out no louder than a mouse's squeak.

Her knees quaked while her head felt close to exploding. The hat she wore—made of whirls of fabric and ribbon piled close to a foot high—weighed upon her head as heavy as an anvil. She raised a trembling hand to swipe her brow as sweat bubbled on her skin. She blinked toward her attorney, but he continued to stare ahead mimicking a statue in a park as he sat halfway twisted toward the judge and the jury. Sparkling pinpricks of light surrounded him like a ghost. She shook her head in hopes of clearing her sight.

How was this possible? The charge of Mayhem. She'd been such a good wife, and here she was charged with a vicious crime not of her own doing. Both parties were at fault—the accused and the accuser—of causing this permanent harm. Misunderstandings, incoherent actions, wild thoughts and nightmares, verbal denigration, and unrelenting anger between two people. Mr. Cruickshank had forewarned her of the charge, but to hear those words spoken aloud brought the weight of a thousand harsh arguments down on her. And now grasping what they meant...*injurious and irreparable harm to another human being.*

Her legs jiggled akin to soupy pudding as they threatened to give out. She had no choice but to grab the edge of the table moments before slumping forward. Her body draped across the table as one arm dangled like a rag-doll over the edge. Her prized hat came loose, fell to the floor, and rolled to a stop in front of the judge's bench. Reminded her of a head severed by a guillotine.

A hat rolling off a bed predicted someone soon to die...so what if a hat fell from a head to a dirty floor? *A death to reflect a miserable life?* Her Grandmother Babcia's words echoed as if the dear woman sat close. Zerelda felt tricked into almost believing moral support had arrived from beyond. Sitting at a kitchen table, laughing together at the shenanigans taking place.

Before darkness tried to overtake her senses, her husband, Narcisco—who sat just a few feet away at the plaintiff's table—blurred before her gaze like petroleum jelly smeared on glass softens the edges. Pain grimaced across his face as he readjusted his position in a similar wooden straight-back chair. Poised and ready as the only victim in this whole charade. Zerelda cheered in silence at his apparent misery, hoping a sooner demise reflected *a miserable life.*

But she was going to be the one to rot in a jail cell. Her attorney, Mr. Cruickshank, had a way of constantly reminding her of that fate even though he'd temper his pessimism with *if convicted.* His lack of confidence fueled her fears of being found guilty. Time off for good behavior had become his chant. But then, who'd ever believe in goodness again when she believed the opposite.

In her fugue state of trying to understand the

A collective quiet blanketed the proceedings; Zerelda even held her breath, waiting for the attorney to continue.

"I will save our defense for the trial as I'm sure there'll be one. My client, Mrs. Zerelda Lena Boronza, pleads not guilty to the charge of Mayhem. She is innocent for reasons beyond her control, and I will prove the truth to the best of my ability."

A split second later, an uproar rose from the gallery. The whooshing sounded like the flapping wings of a hundred blackbirds taking flight. Fruitless beyond the pale, the pounding of the judge's gavel became lost to the rafters. The spectators didn't care about decorum. The judge placed the gavel in front of him, laced his fingers together, and stared out over the crowded room.

Zerelda closed her eyes and prayed for this nightmare scene to end.

Chapter Two

June of 1907, Four Months Earlier

"Woman, where's my coffee." Narcisco's demand screeched worse than a train coming to a halt. Steel wheels on steel rails grinding through her senses.

The empty cup rattled on the bare table, every clack emphasizing a string of never-ending demands; food on the table, coffee always at the ready, service, and slavery. Upon entering the kitchen, he'd sat down to the table, never missing a beat as his gravelly voice intruded Zerelda's thoughts.

She didn't have to look toward him to know how the lock of brown hair dipped down over his forehead before slicking back each strand with pomade, how his deep brown eyes were hooded by eyelashes as thick as a horse's mane, or how the corners of his full lips turned down whenever he had to wait. Or, how he used to put her stomach to roiling in the most pleasant way. And yet, how his grating taunts now killed any desire.

They'd married in 1899. She was twenty-two and in love. He was thirty-four and needed a woman on his arm.

Eight years later, his initial whispers of love and desire had been overshadowed by anger and frustration. Where once they'd walk through town holding hands for all to see with their heads close together talking of growing gardens and a family, insults and impatience grew as insidious as poison ivy. Disappointment festered as more time passed with no children. Where once they'd lie in bed planning parties and trips, silence came. A loneliness crept into their lives as stealthy as fog drifting over a swamp. Laughter had turned to a low growl like a dog guarding its precious bone. No room for two people sharing lives together; solitary confinement in the same house. She wore it like a widow's veil while he suffered as conspicuously as a castrated bull in a field of cows. No way to make him happy anymore.

She turned from the kitchen window, long ago smeared with grimy dust and grease, to face the man she'd learned to hate. After throwing in a dash of salt to take away any bitterness in the coffee, she grabbed the tin pot handle contemplating how magnificent it would be to pour hot coffee over his head. Instead, she yelped. Without a rag in hand, her bare palm sizzled upon contact with the hot metal worse than butter in a hot frying pan. The searing pain caused her hand to splay open and the pot crashed to the floor. Tar-black coffee splattered outward in a circle creating a glorious pinwheel of dots and dashes.

"You turning into a hapless twit, woman?"

"Name's Zerelda," she whispered as her words escaped more like a cough than an answer. She knelt down to retrieve the coffee pot yet paused a moment to flex fingers already stiffening after the hot liquid scalded her skin.

Narcisco threw a towel to the floor for swabbing up the liquid, most of which had already soaked into the greasy black and brown dirt-encrusted wood. Might help the horrible floor if truth be told. No matter how often she swept chunks of dried mud and bits of grain out the back door, the floor always seemed coated with a crunchy layer underfoot. Cleaning had become a useless endeavor. God, if only once this man removed his work boots at the back door instead of traipsing into the kitchen. He treated their home with less respect than his precious barn or the barely-sustainable mill. Polluted house; wicked life together. Hard to tell the difference between the two.

Ella had been their intermediary. Why, oh why, did they let Ella go? She used to make the floor, the rooms, and everything in this whole household clean and orderly. Tension between Narcisco and Zerelda escalated with no one around to encourage politeness. At least with Ella chattering and singing while she worked, casual conversation wasn't necessary.

"Gonna inspect the mill and walk our property today," he continued as if nothing unusual had happened. He even ignored she remained slumped down on her hands and knees scrubbing at a mess never to be polished away. "Gonna be out there most of the day with Ol' Sam. Hope she can handle carrying my tools in this heat, or else that horse is gonna be put out to pasture soon."

Zerelda cringed. "Oh," she exclaimed before covering her mouth. Ol'Sam's future looked dismal if Narcisco had anything to say. Samantha May, nicknamed Ol'Sam, a beautiful yet sway-backed black-and-white speckled mare willingly nuzzled Zerelda's neck as they'd commiserate late at night. But only long after Narcisco had his daily swigs of hooch and fallen asleep by the fire. Many a night after slipping out the back door and into the barn where Ol'Sam munched away at stale hay, Zerelda quietly tossed a few oats into the bin. The horse would move closer and they'd snuggle so their necks came together for warmth and comfort. Dusty misery slithered skyward through the upper loft, forgetting the spent day and hoping for a better one ahead.

The old horse had come to Zerelda from her dear Babcia. When the old woman passed, Zerelda believed a bit of Babcia's soul had transferred to the animal. To help and comfort Zerelda. If only in her thoughts, Babcia's memory held insanity at bay while Zerelda suffered.

"Got...a...problem?" Each drawn-out word of the man's question was enunciated in such a manner to serve as an indictment to her frailties.

"No." Her answer choked past her throat as she struggled up from the floor with her knees protesting at the effort as beads of sweat peppered her face. At thirty years old, she felt worn down, bent over, and used up as much as her dear Babcia had become. Yet right up until the day the old woman died, she'd never stopped showing Zerelda how to value life. Of how a woman can make choices even if told every day she is but a second-class citizen. But now the impossibility of looking at the good in a life gone so horribly wrong seemed as improbable as taking a few tentative steps on the moon. At the rate she'd aged this last year, thirty-one seemed a hopeless goal.

She felt so wretched words could not do justice for the despair she suffered at every turn. Contemplating her unhappiness never produced answers, only melancholy. She'd married this man and dreamed of being the perfect party girl in a glamorous world. His Gibson Girl. He'd made promises she believed.

When they'd married, Zerelda loved everything about the *Naughty Nineties.* Those heady times at the turn of the century when women literally let their hair down. When a Gibson Girl piled her hair as high as possible on her head but left a tail of curls down the middle of her back. When Broadway stretched the limits of decency with shows such as *Floradora* accentuating women's strengths. Zerelda mimicked the star of that scandalous show. Antics and daring fashions no one had ever thought of set into motion everything Zerelda desired. She made promises to Narcisco to be his Gibson Girl. She believed he wanted the same.

Narcisco had swept her off her feet as well. He filled her head with visions of gallantry, glittering ballrooms, loud jazz parties, club-hopping in Detroit, and traveling far and wide. Going across the border into Canada, heading westward toward Chicago, and testing social boundaries dazzled her as much as she him. Over and over, he'd compare Zerelda to voluptuous Broadway actresses yet always claimed they rated a mere second to his gal. She soared, living the life as his Gibson Girl. She worked hard to keep her hourglass figure. She'd style her brown hair in a high coiffure of waves, her eyes were accentuated with dark kohl, and she'd devoured a little bit of something about everything to become a stellar conversationalist. She thrived under his adoration. Flourished through his guidance.

But ultimately, their whirlwind lifestyle disintegrated like crystal drops falling one by one from an uncared-for chandelier. The slide had been gradual at first. Nothing too noticeable. She chose to turn a blind eye to the insidious changes when money began running low. She'd never known or dared to ask where the money came from. Or how, when it did, the well ran dry. Maybe the truth would prove to be more horrible than having the money.

Not unlike her own quiet and unseen slide into oblivion, one such actress's sordid life of sex and murder caused a landslide in public opinion. Covered by New York papers—day after day—her glamorous stature flourished until sensational stories of two men loving the same woman brought it all crashing down. Cedartown readers couldn't get enough of the titillating stories of one man murdering the other—on a rooftop of one of the tallest buildings in New York City, no less—all over the love of a woman.

Zerelda read every account she could find, wanting her story to soar like the actress' even as Narcisco's interest waned. Her tale of glamour fizzled out at the hands of her husband while the actress' career came crashing down because of too much adoration. Similarities between the two were no more wedded than their arrogance before the fall.

When the end came, Zerelda surrendered most of her fancy items to thrift stores. A few things had even been tossed into wanderers' carts as they came around looking for hand-outs. Not much else remained in their house except for a few beaded and laced dresses, broad-rim hats decorated with teal and orange-flecked feathers, some with dried roses ranging from deep red to pale pink to tangerine orange to white. Even fewer bonnets were stacked on top of others where colors matched each outfit, all of varying shapes and sizes and a way to show off her once luxurious hair. A lone pair of champagne-tinted satin mules with pink ribbon trim adorning each top cuff—much too fancy for the dusty roads of Cedartown—stood as a testament to those days. Proof of their extravagances now moldered under a layer of dust like powdery snow.

Black top hats made from silk—never stiff wool like the common man wore—had adorned Narcisco's head as if he were royalty. Silver-tipped canes to loop over his forearm for show stood in a corner as forgotten as Civil War soldiers. Leather shoes to be paired with gray or navy wool suits plus knee-length overcoats and stiff-collar bright-white shirts withered in the armoire from lack of use.

Maybe someday they'd stack the whole mess into the fireplace to warm the house.

Zerelda avoided his finery, choosing to run her roughened fingertips over outdated fashions of her own. Those reminders of an elegant existence hurt as much as enticed.

Ah, but they'd been such a smart couple with each entrance into a restaurant, at a party, or announced while passing under a ballroom archway. Arm-in-arm, they'd parade into any given soiree as if they were the most special couple or thought of as royalty. They expected the highest quality of service by the wait-staff with no questions asked. Other guests bowed to their sophistication and vied for attention. What a heady time. But what a giant fall from the top.

As their resources dwindled, high society turned away, and the shunning stung no less than a million attack bees. Their lives morphed into day after day, hoping farmers brought grain to their mill for processing while living on this poor excuse of a farm...down...stuck in the mud and muck. Now they suffered with only pennies where earlier they'd possessed dollars.

Even if she wanted to play dress-up as his Gibson Girl, she'd lost her verve. The way he treated her with such disrespect and contempt dragged her down to the mud and muck level.

"Oof." Zerelda regained her footing as she grabbed hold of the table and straightened up.

Her dark brown hair ensnared her fingers like a tangle of sticky threads in a spider web. Broken nails scratched her pale skin, and her hazel eyes felt crusted with last night's restless sleep. If only for a hot bath to scrub her skin until every inch shone. She'd use the last sliver of soap—*Marius Fabre Lavender* shea butter— remains of a once-pristine bar given to her by a most entertaining couple in Lansing.

Emmitt and Clara were the consummate host and hostess, and she'd thrilled at such gracious acquaintances. What a treat to be a part of their lives. She and Narcisco had been pressed into spending a night at the couple's house long after guests of a New Year's Eve party had departed instead of them making the long trip back to Cedartown.

"Please, my dear one." Clara had dismissed Zerelda with a wave of a hand. "Take all the shea butter you'd care to have. Dear Emmitt buys those squares of soap by the wagon-load for me." She'd rambled on telling tales of their travels through Europe while Zerelda's insides twittered with envy. "To tell you the truth, dear, luxuries like this are more precious than all the gold and diamonds in the world."

Could this soap work its magic to help resurrect a smidgen of the Gibson Girl she used to be? She gazed down at roughened red hands unfit for anything but scrubbing pots and dishes. Playing the game of *if only* they'd saved half of what they'd squandered, socked away a bit of gold or a diamond or two, or been better to others never did her any good. But she played it anyhow.

"Heading downtown later today," Narcisco muttered under his breath. "Want to walk with me?"

She startled at his near-civil invitation as a flutter of appreciation worked through her nerve-endings, reminding her of days gone by. Was there enough time to bathe? She'd make time to unsnarl her hair after soaking it with an egg yolk and Borax mixture while the water warmed on the stove. A touch of peppermint oil to the baking soda and salt for brushing her teeth was in order. As she ran her tongue over stale front teeth, she wondered at the last time she'd done even the simplest bit of pampering.

She'd make time or be damned trying.

They rarely left this hovel as a couple. A few heads would probably turn at the sight of them together but maybe not for the reason she hoped for. Some probably even wondered if she still lived with Narcisco. He'd inherited the ramshackle house, mill, and land from his parents, and during the intervening years, an invisible leash had tethered her within the hopeless confines. The house had become an eyesore. He'd leave unfinished chores all too often to spend precious daylight hours at the firehouse. After starting out as a volunteer—more a lark than a passion—the village council gave him a small pittance from their coffers to run the haphazard

shoulder blades creating a tail like an upside-down question mark. The trademark of the perfect Gibson Girl as immortalized in charcoal sketches.

"Wake up, woman." Narcisco's snarl resounded throughout the kitchen. "Are you coming with me or goin' to waste away the day sitting there. Call you a queen from now on."

Zerelda jerked back to the present and banged her kneecap hard against the rough wood of one of the legs supporting the kitchen table. Tears gathered at the corners of her eyes as she gulped down a yelp of pain. When she brought her gaze up to Narcisco, though, she startled at the scene over his shoulder. Thick black smoke billowed behind him outside beyond the doorway and kitchen window.

She tried to focus by blinking away threatening tears. Something burned not far from the house. As she raised her hand to point toward the mill, Narcisco must have also caught a whiff of acrid smoke. He turned and ran out the kitchen door before either of them uttered a sound. His suspenders flapped like loosened bridle straps as he jumped from foot to foot, trying to settle into his boots.

She limped to the kitchen door, trying to ignore her knee. The pain screamed through her thoughts as if the kneecap had been pounded flat. Narcisco disappeared as the smoke swallowed him up as ferocious as a starving dragon. Flames scourged up the south side of the three-story building, and the fire bell a block away was clanging so loud the noise sounded to be next door. The bucket brigade arrived within minutes. Rats rushed from the building as angry flames licked at their backsides, causing the men to dance around them.

Zerelda stood mesmerized by the stampede of dark brown rodents streaming out from the base of the mill as the glow from the flames lit the animals' backs an orange tinge. No sense even trying to count how many fled the building as the majority charged toward the house looking for refuge from the heat.

If a bird loose in the house is a sign of death, a rat foretells suffering.

She stepped back inside and slammed the door so hard the glass in the kitchen window shattered, causing large shards to cascade into the house and outside down to the weeds below. If the rats were along the rock foundation of the house, they'd scale their way upward and in through the newly-created gap. She grabbed a couple pots from the stove and started banging the bottoms together, making a racket so loud her ears rang in dissonant notes.

She paused. Zerelda waited for one of those rodents to peek in through the frame, but none appeared. Without waiting longer, she banged the pots together a few more times and then braced herself against the sink edge in order to push up and peer out the window. Nothing appeared to be scrambling up the clapboard siding, but the green tangle of weeds and wild grasses swayed as if a strong wind had caught the blades. Even if the stampede was hidden from her view, she knew those rats were there.

She eased back down and gulped air into her lungs—a swimmer breaking the water's surface to breathe again. Her throat stung from the dark smoke filtering in through the window. As quick as her shaking legs worked, she climbed up on to the edge of the sink to drape a couple towels over the opening. The temporary curtains helped to slow the insidious smoke from entering. Her senses returned long enough to realize the sound of the fire bell no longer clanged in the distance.

This meant one of two scenarios. They'd contained the fire with not too much damage or—and this she feared the most—hope had burned up along with the barn. She watched the dejected men standing as witness to the loss of most of the building, and then they shuffled away from the destruction of Narcisco's and her livelihood. She nervously tapped her knuckles on the wooden table knowing full well evil had visited them and the disastrous scene furthered their dire state of affairs, and wondered how Narcisco would respond.

Chapter Three

July of 1907, Nights Spent Alone

"Heading out to the firehouse," Narcisco mumbled.

He grabbed his outerwear off the hook by the back door and slid the wool coat over his shoulders, enveloping him larger than a horse blanket over a pony. He slunk a battered hat low over his brow. His eyes disappeared behind the shadow of the brim as he turned toward the door. Narcisco looked like he'd shrunken since the fire a few weeks back.

"Not going to wait around for dinner?" Zerelda stood in front of the wood-burning stove as she moved a ladle throughout the soup in a figure-eight pattern. The spoon continued its path around and around.

Shadows were growing long outside, and these were the first words they'd spoken to each other all day. She didn't care one way or the other whether he stayed for a meal. By now, conversations had become non-existent. The three days after the fire at the mill, they'd spoken plenty. Arguments swirled around...

...how she must have left a lantern burning for Ol'Sam...

...how a careless toss of one of his foul-smelling cigars at a bin must have started it...

...how her idiotic superstitions must have brought disaster...

…how his monstrous attitude cursed them…

…how she'd become spoiled…

Then silence. Throughout the few weeks, mumbling answers to stilted questions had barely broken the museum-like silence.

Earlier in the day, they'd gone their separate ways. He headed to the building skeleton to continue tearing away at the charred beams. Two-thirds of the structure stood and had escaped the flames thanks to the hard work of the water brigade. Eighteen men had lined up from the shoreline of a small creek that meandered like a snake along the north side of the mill to within a few feet of the hot fire. They'd passed along bucket after bucket of water sloshing and spilling to then be emptied and returned back down the line.

Hot time in the old mill, slow the fire from going downhill.

The chant went on repeatedly even as exhaustion etched every man's face and soot seeped into sweaty pores to skim down wrinkles in black rivulets. A muddy pile of charred timbers came to rest at the feet of a few sturdy beams reaching skyward but of no use any longer.

In the end, Zerelda escaped the only way she knew how. She'd pinned on her best going-to-church bonnet—as if praying might help more than her superstitions—and walked the couple of blocks to Mr. Navarro's grocery store. She picked up needed food supplies all but forgotten about when the fire broke out.

The senseless arguments wore her down. They'd never know why or how the fire flared up, but she worked hard to dispel the bitter taste of this setback. Chicken soup had been her solution, but he didn't want to wait around. The bubbles percolating upward in the broth were mesmerizing as she breathed in the steam. A mere hint of the smoke stench remained. The chicken simmering amongst carrots and potatoes with extra salt and a healthy dose of pepper almost dispelled the musty odor. Mr. Navarro had even thrown in a stalk of celery for her to use—said something about not wanting produce to wilt. She'd graciously accepted the gift.

"What to do?" She spoke out loud, knowing full well no one would answer. The ping of the metal ladle on the pot rang a reminder of the two pan bottoms she'd used to scare away vermin. At least in those few moments, she'd been successful. But now, something worse slithered serpent-like through this house. No matter how hard she tried, Narcisco's scowl never left his face. Agreeing to disagree didn't work, nor finding some humor in how the rats proved defenseless against a crazy woman banging out a tune of discontent with a fistful of pots and pans.

Maybe sitting around a table with other men in the firehouse reliving their most exciting fire-fighting escapades might make a difference in his mood.

Even as humid air descended on the village and frayed at nerves, the taste of the soup on her lips eased a tension roiling within. Even took her mind to thoughts of refreshing her collection of hats. Or pledging to wear them more often. No respectable woman left the confines of home without proper headwear while in public. She'd wear her best even when she was gardening if it helped her to hold her head high and preempt possible judgment.

Villagers seemed to have short memories. She and Narcisco had suffered the sting of being shunned not too long ago, and now they were the recipients of care and concern and generosity. A great comfort of donated meals had kept them fed. Some of the ladies in town knew of her love for creating high-profile hats and had sorted through long-forgotten fabric. A basketful of silk and satin scrap offerings with streamers of tulle had shown up at their side door. Was it the ladies' way of scaring off heartache from landing at their own doorsteps? To stave off a tragic fire, illness, or rumors of desertion?

Either way, Zerelda's gratefulness for the gifts helped give her motivation and to savor the opportunity of being proud of her gorgeous hats once more. A small blessing she'd view as a lifeline.

She slurped the warm soup with a bit more gusto and savored the saltiness on her tongue as the warm liquid soothed her still-ragged throat. Thoughts continued to swirl around her head of winding the deep purple tulle seductively around mauve satin roses. Each item would be delicately placed on a wide-brimmed platform to stand a healthy six or more inches above the crown of her head. The whole effect created a statuesque feel to her slim five-foot height. And yet, even with her favorite hat poised atop her head, Narcisco still towered above her.

Dusk blanketed the village and brought a slowing to the day and a calmness to her musings. With no urgency at hand, she roused from the kitchen table, placed the spent bowl in the soapy water, and struck a match to light the oil lamp over the cutting board. Their last argument crept into her thoughts. She'd extinguished the lantern in the barn. She was certain. Ol'Sam had snorted and sputtered in the eerie flickering light of flames until one of the men came to her rescue. In her heart, she questioned if Narciso had somehow created this problem. Of his making, some of the local ladies must have found a certain pleasure in their pretense of feeling sorry for her. He didn't seem to be the beneficiary as much as she had become. Had her thinking something didn't quite add up right.

She fingered the scratchy tulle fabric before going in search of her favorite bonnet as well as needle and thread. She worked long into the night by the soft light of the flickering oil lamp. She wrapped, turned, twisted, and manipulated fabric around the roses to create a continuous flow of color from the beginning all the way around to tucking in loose ends.

Zerelda cared very little of Narciso's absence by the time she crawled under the covers. Thoughts kept her tossing and turning. Why didn't he just do her a favor and walk away, or…

…disappear on foot down the dirt road carrying no more than an extra shirt and a pistol.

…plod away on the back of the only workhorse leaving the abandoned with nothing.

…board a train for parts unknown and head west in search of elusive gold.

…find another to love.

…place a pistol to his own temple and pull the trigger.

…dangle as lifeless as fresh-killed deer from a frayed rope secured to a massive beam in the old barn.

Ocean waves of worry washed over her that he would make any of those choices, but she fussed more of him falsely accusing her of adultery. Gossip always spread through small towns like wildfire whether true or not. She'd have been leered at by men, robbed of her good name, alienated by other women, or deprived of any standing in the community. She'd lost all sensibility of what he was capable of doing.

****

Narcisco stayed away all the next day.

Zerelda thought she spotted him walking around toward the east side of the half-standing mill building, but he'd disappeared with a quickness that surprised her. She couldn't be certain what she saw. Maybe dusty ghosts were rising up from the rubble. So engrossed in working the needle in and out of the fabric, she ignored his absence. She found contentment working a matching shade of mauve thread to the fabric making the stitches invisible when the flowers were secured. Gave her more satisfaction than worrying about an absentee husband.

When he stayed away another night, though, her mind began playing tricks filled with dark suspicions. Sullen thoughts of being left to fend for herself. Never did she spot an advertisement in the local newspaper of a wife throwing out a husband; the announcement almost always made the husband out to be the victim. Some went so far as to stop a *disobedient* wife from being able to purchase much-needed supplies by accusing her of abandonment when it was the husband that had left. Would have been more satisfying to see a bordered advert in the classified section announcing, *Ladies! I threw out my husband. You can too. For $1, I'll teach you!*

Narcisco's face never used to show his love or dislike; a mask hid his true feelings. She never had absolute faith in how he felt. Her confidence wavered even during their heady and glorious times of treating money like candy. Now the helplessness wavered over her as their cursed and pauper lives emphasized his meanness.

The worn mattress and soft bedding beckoned her by the time midnight rolled around. As she tossed and turned, wondering if he'd ever come home, sleep eluded her. She'd convinced herself he'd found another woman, and the time had come to confront him. She'd not be left homeless, helpless, or at the mercy of some shop owner to take pity on her. He would pay for his cruelty—somehow.

****

Oh, how she hates me. Words thrown across the room as vicious as daggers. I only slept at the firehouse to give her time to appreciate me. Not to continue to accuse me of wrong-doing. What have I done to this woman she cannot find forgiveness in her heart to believe in me? How my intentions are honorable toward her, yet how much disdain can one man take? Regrettably, I may have to search hard for a reason to stay.

The next morning Narcisco slumped down to the kitchen table after Zerelda had stormed out the back door, slinging a few more choice words unbefitting a lady. Surprise worked through him that she even knew such language. No doubt she'd find solace crying into Ol'Sam's mane. The burned mill was their burden to share, yet her temper accentuated how wrong he'd been leaving her alone. He should have stayed here to reassure her they'd rebuild and be more profitable than before.

The townsfolk had said as much. When the mill

27

became operational again, they'd spread the word across the county for farmers to use his grinders, benefit from his experience, and to get the best pricing. He began imagining money piling up better than before he'd lost interest in the mill.

I am ready to fight for what we had. But she has to meet me part way. If not, there are a dozen other women lining up I could choose from. Does she know that or even care?

Chapter Four

August of 1907, Elusive Answers

Never before in her life had Zerelda imagined knocking on such a door.

Words stenciled across the glass glared with accusation at her—*Private Investigator*—as if she had done something wrong. The mauve-colored lettering matched Zerelda's favorite hat, and that alone gave her courage to step closer to read the name *Corey Strayer* above the stated occupation.

The strength of that color triggered her knuckles to pound harder than planned. The window in the door rattled as a bell strung from the knob jingled, and she stepped back for fear of breaking something more in her life. She paused. Did manners predicate to walk right into the office, or should she wait to be admitted? In the big city, she felt everyone moved at a bolder and noisier pace than in Cedartown. So much different from a small village, causing her self-confidence to suffer now.

"Enter."

The deep baritone voice sounded muffled through the door, causing Zerelda to look at the signage again. She didn't know whether Corey was a man or a woman. She did not want to tell her story to a man; her only real experience being of gossip leaked by the small-town *hawkshaw* in their village. She pulled her hand away from the door wishing she could take back the knock and wavered as to entering or to escape.

Before making up her mind one way or another, though, the door yawned open, presenting a vestibule barely large enough for two people. Zerelda stood face-to-face with a rather tall woman. Tall by Zerelda's standards but also appearing even more imposing by the clothes Corey Strayer wore. If not for her hair wrapped up in a beautiful bun with a few dainty curls encasing her face, Zerelda might have thought a man stood before her.

Zerelda had never before seen in person a woman wearing slacks and a high-collared dress shirt. The only items of clothing missing to make her more manly-looking might have been a cravat at her neck, and an overcoat draped over her shoulders. Walking down any city street, a person might mistake her for a man. What a surprise awaited someone looking close enough at her! Zerelda's thoughts went to the fact a bonnet on this woman's head had the ability to create a sensation on the streets of Cedartown. Maybe here in Lansing many tolerated differences, but she'd make quite the splash in their small town. Without question, it would be scandalous. Gossip wouldn't die down for a month.

Seconds stretched between them as Miss Strayer's eyebrows rose in question.

No turning back now. Zerelda needed to find out what or who her husband had gotten involved with. After a brief stop at their house to pick at pieces of the worn-out argument as cruel as coyotes tearing at the last chunks of a dead animal, Narcisco had disappeared. Enough was enough.

Once she'd made her decision, she'd sold two of her most prized and largest hats to Mr. Hamilton in town. Though she let both go for far less than their worth, she was able to purchase a round-trip train ticket to Lansing. The next day she boarded the ten o'clock train westward to Lansing to unearth a private investigator. Finding a confidante in Cedartown would be like trying to find one of her needles in Ol' Sam's hay feed. Especially with the only detective that town had to offer being a scurrilous *hawkshaw* with shifty eyes and a slimy brashness. He called himself an attorney but keeping one's secret and lacking discretion served as a strange code of conduct. Such a gossip when he had a salacious tidbit to pass along. And he always acted so superior to her. Her being a woman. Plus, didn't men stick together? For all she could imagine, Benjamin Walton would have trailed hot on her heels out of his office and headed for the firehouse to report Zerelda's inquiry.

"Going to stare all day or come in and tell me what you need." The woman spoke as if no moment need be wasted with indecision or pleasantries.

So here she stood, thirty-odd miles from home, nervous to make the two o'clock train back to Cedartown, and not sure how a woman investigating from so far away might work. A fool's errand. If only she had thought of this before.

"Ma'am, I don't have all day to stand here holding this door open for you."

"Oh, my yes, yes, I realize…" Zerelda stammered. She made up her mind in the blink of an eye. "I need to hire you."

"Now we are getting somewhere."

Zerelda stepped into the tight front room, not uttering another word. Corey Strayer then opened yet another door and strolled into a large office. Zerelda peeked around the doorframe to see a richly-polished walnut desk dwarfing even the investigator as she sat down. Glass cabinets on opposing walls were crammed tight with books; some volumes standing up, others tossed on their bellies or spread wide open, and even more stacked on the floor alongside the monstrous pieces of furniture. Two rather uncomfortable-looking chairs were positioned in front of the desk. The worn forest green brocade fabric had faded at the center of each seat and the arms as if a thousand clients had sat whispering their stories of woe. Or pounding the arms in violent frustration.

The investigator indicated for Zerelda to take a seat in one of those chairs. She did, placing her satchel on the floor and making to remove her hat.

"Oh no, leave the hat on," Corey rushed her comment. "My dear, most becoming. I'm enjoying how the fabric shimmers in the light whenever you move your head."

Niggling doubts lessened for Zerelda. She'd come this far; no going back. Maybe this woman would accept the hat as payment since coins were at a premium. She had plenty of fabric remaining in the basket back at home to make any style of hat she desired.

"Now tell me, how can I help you?"

"Well...I don't trust my husband."

"Can't help you with trust."

"I'm saying it wrong. I want to find out what he does at night. I believe he's making to leave me,"

Zerelda said as unexpected tears threatened to fall. This untenable situation she found herself involved in weighed heavy. She and Narcisco argued day in and day out with barely a civil word spoken, or they ignored each other, and yet she remained convinced his abandonment would leave her destitute.

"Are you afraid of being branded deserted?"

"Yes, most certainly," she replied to the blunt question. "I don't want to appear as a failure. To be ridiculed and made to feel like a pariah. Although I don't know which is worse—abandonment or divorce. At least when someone leaves, there's hope of a return."

"You're telling me appearances are as important as actually having a husband," Corey pondered. "Do you agree?"

"No. I'm not sure. I've never cared what anyone thinks of me." Zerelda leaned forward. Corey made Zerelda feel—more than anything at this moment—to impart her greatest secrets to a person she didn't know a thing about. "All I've ever wanted...all I've ever dreamt of...having a grand time. And we were. Now we have so little, and townsfolk will think he left me because I stuck around for the good times. But I wasn't..." She couldn't go on. When said out loud how they had reveled in the good times and now how they were so at odds made it sound like all she ever meant to him was as...

"A prize," Corey spoke up. She'd finished Zerelda's comment, hitting a bull's eye dead center.

"When you describe me in such a way," Zerelda responded, "crass comes to mind. I fail to believe I've been nothing more than a prize. But...maybe that's how

balconies and stone edifices provided sample rooms where salesmen showed off their wares. The building stood one block from the firehouse, three blocks from Narcisco and Zerelda's house, and at the main four corners of the village where no activity went unnoticed since 1878. Thirty years of gossip and rumors and nosiness for everybody's consumption.

"I'm wondering," Corey queried as she'd escorted Zerelda to the office entrance, "why did you come to me instead of finding someone closer to home?"

"Because of my right foot."

Corey had tilted her head to the left grazing a second bell bolted to the door frame. A pleasant ding echoed. "Your foot."

"Oh yes," Zerelda had answered, remembering Babcia's life philosophy of following one's intuition. "I knew the moment my right foot took to being itchy I had better get ready for a trip."

Corey hadn't replied nor asked another question, her response being to politely nod and assure Zerelda she'd be in touch.

And now, as Zerelda strolled along Michigan Avenue toward the train station, she allowed a slight smile to grace her expression. A few passing women raised puzzling eyebrows in her direction, no doubt because of her bare head—going hatless being a notable social faux pas—while the gents tipped their bowlers toward her.

Her thoughts sobered and slowed her steps. She needed to be patient; wait to hear from Corey. To not let on to Narcisco anything might be amiss.

She had to be strong, capable of holding this at bay. Babcia would remind her *loneliness comes with keeping secrets*. Yet, for once, her grandmother might have been wrong. This secret could take away the loneliness she'd been living with for far too long.

Chapter Five

September of 1907, Once Upon a Saleslady

Corey inclined her head toward Zerelda just enough no one would have noticed unless they were looking for it.

They passed each other on the sidewalk in front of Hamilton's building. It was the exact type of dry goods store Corey had described for her client as their plan of action took shape. A slight smile creased Zerelda's lips, but the investigator frowned to indicate secrecy.

A couple weeks had passed since the Commercial Hotel became their base of operation, and Corey set up one of the sample rooms as a cover. She looked the part of a salesperson, having brought a trunk full of ladies' clothing, undergarments, and lacy linens as examples. Zerelda had asked if some were her own personal items but didn't question the frillier pieces. Little did she know the bonnet had enticed Corey enough to go purchase a few more feminine articles for herself. They made for a great display for now.

No one came to check on the samples, but no matter.

Zerelda had stepped into the room a couple of times after making sure no one lingered in the hallway to notice. She and Corey talked of any new developments whenever they had these few moments.

Corey's task, so far, had been unsuccessful in learning anything solid in Narcisco's activities. She did laughingly call his actions curious, a bit bizarre, and even a little boring. He spent a great deal of time at the firehouse, but, more often, he wandered the village streets before ending up at the mill. He'd opt for a few hours rebuilding the destroyed portion instead of coming into the house. He never appeared to be in a hurry but disappeared for long periods. The man strutted around—acting as if without a care—and Corey questioned these actions to Zerelda. She'd just shrug her shoulders and be noncommittal of not having a clue if anything was normal for Narcisco, and any speculation on her part didn't seem helpful.

If Corey took on a client, she had to believe in that person. Trust they honestly felt wronged. The hallmark of her philosophy revolved around believing the person showing up at her doorstep. Any lack of trust ultimately lay between her client and the person being investigated. She'd felt an immediate kinship with Zerelda.

Women's intuition had only recently been recognized as having any relevancy and was gaining minimal credibility. With advancements, though, came derision from those nonbelievers. Corey had long ago figured out paying attention to her own thoughts, how her insides repelled or felt drawn to someone, or getting a good night's sleep as opposed to suffering nightmares gave her more answers than puzzles. Corey listened to her twittering gut during the first meeting with Zerelda as the woman believed evil had entered her life. And if a person is a true believer, trust is tricky. The strand between two people can be as strong as a million silken threads of a spider web or as tenuous as disappearing smoke rings.

Corey knew about such heartache and always kept her hurt locked in the back of her mind to prevent another cut so deep. Sadness drained energy, and self-worth suffered where once she trusted and believed in happily ever after. But never again. It had been five years ago her world came crashing down.

The ceremony had been simple and short, held in her parents' living room, with the minister happy to imbibe on the punch and munch on enough snacks afterward to be his dinner. A week-long train ride to Arizona was capped meeting her new husband's folks. It had been sublime. Not having any idea how a visit with new in-laws would be, she still congratulated herself for appearing to live up to their standards. They all reveled in spirited conversations, elegant dinners with their friends, and hikes amongst the jumping cholla, statuesque saguaros, and spiny prickly pear cactus as they spoke of their future. Two weeks in that desert state filled up a lifetime of happy-ever-after.

But upon their return to Lansing, her faith in men was eviscerated. Her marriage failed as quickly as it began. She'd been sent reeling across a canyon of grief.

Against her better instincts earlier, she entertained positive thoughts and ignored a blaring twist in her gut. To wait and get to know the man better. She forged ahead with the wedding and the trip. Next on their list, a blissful new married life in Michigan.

Until…

Until she discovered her newly-minted husband had a whole and complete family—even a passel of adorable rambunctious children—across town where he'd split his time between them and her. Devastation hit like an avalanche. His betrayal gutted any belief of self-worth she had before the moment his other wife showed up at her doorstep to demand Corey give up this charade. From that moment on, she was on the warpath to never let a man's ill-treatment of a woman go unpunished, if she had any say in the matter.

A judge had granted her a divorce quicker than predicted. Corey argued her own case, bringing to light the first divorce in the United States happened back two hundred and fifty years ago when a man wouldn't go back to his wife after fathering two children with another woman. The wife was granted legal rights over her own sovereignty in the face of abandonment and such stubborn behavior on the man's part.

Her mission then became clear—as long as she had the ability to right such a wrong, to mend a broken heart, or to make the bloody bastard suffer, she'd do her best.

Corey also figured out how to work an angle enabling her to change lives wronged by the male ego's selfishness. With each injustice brought to light, he paid a price for her silence. Blackmail is such a horrid word yet so effective. If a man worried his name might be smeared across the front page as a no-good slime of a grafter taking advantage of unsuspecting women, he paid up. If he wanted to ensure her silence being absolute, a few additional deposits were given in kind. If she proved successful in burying his unsavory actions, she might find gift boxes mysteriously showing up inside the office vestibule.

She never backed out on any deal. Once a man proved himself a generous rapscallion, he gained a trusted colleague in her. His questionable reputation stayed hidden. At least by her. She'd laugh in her more private moments how convoluted this practice had become as irony abounded. But it only made her press harder. And she had an excellent system to insure her worth.

All of those men understood evidence existed of their behavior but not how or where the information was stashed. Each envelope contained a complete run-down of the deceitful act. The lawyer she'd employed had instructions for how even the most minuscule detail would see the light of day if anything unseemly happened to her.

Corey told Zerelda—a woman lacking of any resources other than her beautiful bonnets—coinage wasn't necessary. Men long before her had paid the price as they would into the future. Their guilt funded making a woman safer or happier. Some men may have even been brought back from the brink to bask in the benefits of saving both money and their reputation.

Corey fingered the bonnet's edge as it balanced atop her tightly-wrapped bun of hair and stayed in place secured by a silky sash bow under her chin. She enjoyed the trim feel of the brim with pins tucked out of sight while the fabric swayed with her every step. She nodded a second time at Zerelda and continued toward the firehouse. Her plan involved inquiring as to the security of the lockup in case she apprehended someone trying to abscond with her samples.

****

Corey batted her eyes at the young man. It had been a long time since she felt the need to flirt, but this felt so nice. She couldn't resist running her tongue over moistened lips rubbed red with a rouge cream. She even placed both hands on her hips and pushed her bosom upward in a stance that might be enticing, if not a bit uncomfortable.

He rocked from one foot to the other as if being a moving target helped him figure out how to talk to a woman. Something seemingly foreign to him. A rosy blush worked up into his cheeks, not unlike a young teenage girl. She almost felt sorry for him.

After surveying the wide-open firehouse with the sheriff's operation off to one side by the jail cells and the northeast corner containing stacks of books looking a lot like a library, she'd asked to see the lockup. Refusal had been quick and emphatic. Said the men's cells weren't something meant for a lady to see. Although his reply sounded more along the lines, "ain't no place for a lady," as he hawked a line of spittle toward the hay-covered floor.

"But," she began, "I need to know there will be no worries for me."

"No one's ever escaped if you're askin'," he reiterated. "They tried but failed. One prisoner darn near froze. He thought settin' a couple blankets on fire right inside the cage would help him escape after warmin' his feet and hands and gettin' us to unlock the door. Near 'bout burned hisself behind them bars."

"But I'm but a woman, defenseless on my own," Corey cooed, moving one step closer to him. "I want to make sure, as I travel with my wares, no one will steal them. If someone does try, will you protect me?"

"You need to talk to Fire Chief Boronza," the young man replied. "He's not the sheriff, but he'll tell you the same, and he's supposed to be right back."

Corey hadn't expected the conversation to take that direction. While talking with the sheriff, she'd hoped to observe her mark if Narcisco was in the building. She'd been ready to confront him to see if her assessment matched Zerelda's fears. But this was happening faster than a scared rabbit skittering off a different way.

The main door from where she'd entered moments earlier squeaked open. Easy enough for her to make an excuse about coming back later. None of this had been part of the plan, but she always chose flexibility to reach her goal. She threw her shoulders back and smiled—it was now or never to try this new flirting ability with him to evaluate his response.

"What do we have here?"

The young man she'd been talking with took a couple tentative steps backward and scraped a hand across darkening stubble on his chin. He trained his gaze at the floor as he turned away from her, acting as guilty as one snitching a cookie from the pantry.

Corey knew who stood inches just inside the door. An odor of a long-ago extinguished cigar hovered at her back, smelling like someone had walked through brackish gray ash at a burned-out mill building. She plastered a most ingratiating smile and turned toward the husband Zerelda feared laid with another woman. She towered over him by at least two, maybe three, inches, and he even seemed to shrink more as she looked down upon the top of his head. Her hat made her height over him even more impressive.

As he looked her up and down, a lush sweep of brown hair held in place with musky pomade never moved. Looked like carved marble as a dim light from above reflected off the grease. He'd walked in hatless—

unusual for a man in 1907—giving him a squattier look.

As she contemplated his lacking appearance, he stared hard at her bonnet. This gave her a moment to gather thoughts scattering throughout the room faster than a dust devil.

"You must be Mr. Boronza," she carefully stated. "Do I have your name correct? This young man has been so gracious as to inform me I need to speak with you regarding the integrity of your lockup."

One of Narcisco's eyebrows arched in a sideways question mark. The expression caused the left side of his face to lift unevenly from the right side. Not so much a sneer but more a toady glare of disapproval. Some may consider him handsome—more so than Zerelda had described him—but his eyes held back secrets. The man looked elsewhere. Over to the lockup to where the sheriff usually sat, to the hoses, to the buckets placed at the ready for the next fire, but he avoided eye contact with her.

"I am," he responded. "But I'm sorry to say the lockup is not available for visitors. Now"—and here he smirked—"if you'd care to commit a crime, I'd be more than happy to have Sheriff Calkins show you the insides of our spacious accommodations."

"No-o-o," she answered, scoffing at his cocky attitude. She waved her hand around as if chasing after a pesky fly. Him included. "I'm more concerned I and my wares be safe in this little village of yours during my stay."

"And how long will you be gracing us with your presence?"

Oh, what a smooth one that good *ol'cox-comb.* So vain, all she saw was ugly. No wonder Zerelda

offered. Shunned, shut out, destitute…unless the woman had another man waiting to help.

"If he comes home tonight, I will confront him. Another argument will be no worse than the horrific words we've said to each other these last few weeks."

"I have watched him for two weeks. I will stay longer if you need me to, but if not, I'll be on the one o'clock train back to Lansing."

Corey offered up a small smile and shrugged her shoulders upward. Zerelda felt a bit abandoned, and she wavered in her conviction. But as positive as she could be the sun would rise tomorrow, her instincts still screamed Narcisco to be wicked. There must be a way to find out. And now dreadful thoughts consumed all else of him making plans to leave. Terrified of being left behind made her fear life might become all the harder to bear. A stranded woman depended on the kindness of others in this small village. And how some treated her, she questioned if compassion would land on her front door. The show of charity within days of the fire had disappeared as swift as the flames had licked up the sides of the mill structure.

"I will talk with him tonight *if* he comes home," Zerelda answered. She took a bite of one of the biscuits, and a piece clogged in her throat, making her cough. She dabbed away the threat of tears as she choked down disappointment and crumbs. She cleared her throat after pushing down the last bit with a rather large gulp of tea. "Let's talk about something else now."

"Before we do, may I ask one more question?" Corey waited for Zerelda's nod. "Do you think any of his actions have something to do with figuring out why the mill burned?"

Chapter Six

September of 1907, Unintended Consequences

"You sellin' hats?"

Zerelda jumped at Narcisco's question—both because he'd startled her out of thoughts so deep his entrance into the room had gone undetected and because his accusatory tone bristled at her senses. She steeled already raw nerves for yet another battle of words.

"Woman, did you hear me? You…selling…hats?"

"I heard you the first time," she responded, after a lengthy silence. "Why do you ask?"

"I'm asking for my own reasons."

"What reason?" She had to stall him or wheedle more information out of him before giving a wrong answer. Her breathing came in short puffs as dread snaked through her body. She didn't dare stand up from the chair she'd been occupying while doing some knitting for fear of wobbly legs crumpling under her.

"Don't have to tell you any reason," he responded. "But so's you know, saw a woman wearing a hat looked same as one of yours."

"Looked similar to one of mine or was?"

"Hell, I don't know, woman. You've got so many of those contraptions. Who bothers to keep track?"

"How does any of this matter to us?"

"I want to know if you're selling hats. The mill's 'bout back in operation, and money's coming in from the firehouse. I don't need anyone saying I don't take care of my own."

"Who'd ever spread such rumors?" Something to latch onto and move away from his questioning. Corey Strayer had mentioned how much she loved her new bonnet and coordinating outfits with the luscious mauve colors. Made for fun detecting as she fashionably scoured the village for dirt on Narcisco. But now, they may have caused him to be suspicious.

"Just talk I hear. Seems there's nothing else for the gossips to talk about."

"Well...I hear talk too." Zerelda waited to see if Narcisco would rise to the bait.

He'd been standing two steps inside the archway from the dining room to the front parlor. Anger spread across his face, but he also acted as guilty as an escapee from the jail. Looked like he was ready to bolt either toward the bedroom or out the back door.

"What kind?" he demanded. He curled his lips downward in a cruel sneer.

"Maybe not so much talk, but I notice your actions. You don't look me in the eyes when we talk. I never know if you're coming home at night or if I'd be better off shooting you like some drifter breaking in. And tell me, where are you getting money to rebuild the mill? Or if you are walking away from all of this...and me."

"You've gone daft, woman," he replied. His hand went to his head to smooth back a lock of hair separating itself from the rest of his perfectly-oiled hair. His fingers shook and proved ineffective as a couple more strands came loose, giving him an unkempt look.

The man standing before her screamed of fleeing as he clenched his fists, glared at her, and took another step backward toward the door.

"I dreamt..."

"Stop. I don't want to hear about all your superstitions."

Zerelda waited a heartbeat for him to continue, but he'd gone quiet. "I dreamt the other night you were behind those bars at the lockup. Want to know what that tells me?" She gave him another second to back out of the room, but his feet appeared stuck to the floor. "Means you are deceitful and untrustworthy. That you are putting a barrier between us to create distance, and you're going to leave me because you feel confined and suffocated. Am I close?"

"Do you want to be alone?"

"You afraid to answer me? I asked you a question first. You planning on running off with some other woman and leaving me to fend for myself?"

"I repeat...you've gone daft."

"Tell me you haven't been thinking about leaving," she demanded. With no thought of consequences, her legs responded as anger coursed through her body. She stood and moved to the center of the room, so the only thing between them was a guest chair next to a little three-legged side table. "Tell me you aren't thinking of leaving me, all this putting the mill back together isn't some game you're playing to make me think different, and that spending all your time at the firehouse isn't the best part of this marriage."

Silence. Except for her own hot breath wheezing past her throat. Her chest rose and collapsed as she gulped in stale air and tried to make sense of the man

51

standing before her, not saying one single word.

He spun on his heels and left the house through the back door before she expanded her lungs enough to scream at him. She did have the strength, though, to throw a wooden knitting needle through the archway. With dagger-like precision, it sailed past the dining table and clattered to the floor not far from his leg a split second before he disappeared into the dark.

Zerelda felt nothing but emptiness throughout the entire house. Those words were never to be unspoken, and now Corey Strayer's investigations had been for naught. Narcisco had his own plans, those not including her. Realization hit her as hard as a breath-stealing punch between the shoulder blades...she had to take action.

****

"Hot time in the old meal...mill...slow the fire from going down my heel...downhill," Narcisco sang as he swayed side to side and grabbed hold of the doorframe to steady himself. "In the old mill, not damn meal. Down the hill. Not down my heel..." He giggled but stopped short, bringing a stubby finger to his lips to shush his singing. The drink had gone so far to his head his mouth felt full of cotton, and his eyes might as well roll back into his skull for what little good they were doing.

He stood at the kitchen doorway surveying his crumbling kingdom before him. He'd just come from the half-rebuilt mill, in all its shame, standing as a testament of how he continued to fail those around him. He knew how the fire started, but he'd continue to hide the truth. He knew how the flames smoldered off to one corner from a lit cigar placed by his own hand under a mound of straw and grain. He cringed, remembering how he'd hurriedly left the building to be sitting at the kitchen table demanding coffee of his wife before any smoke slithered skyward.

And only he knew the why.

He alone knew changing the course from wrong to right with his wife of nearly ten years weighed on his shoulders. But stupid pride, bad choices, and his own arrogance stood in front of him like a stone wall too tall to scale. The sad part was he felt pretty certain fixing the problem wasn't even worth the effort.

Chapter Seven

September of 1907, Under the Cover of Darkness

Zerelda stood at the entrance to their bedroom.

Narcisco's lips twitched with each slow intake and exhale of air. Her nose wrinkled at the stale air ripe with rye mash alcohol. It was as cloying as a cellar full of decaying apples gone mushy and moldering to chunky thick cider.

She moved the straight razor from one hand to the other. Oil had routinely been brushed onto the blade to prevent rusting, which made her palm feel slimy as it smeared from the handle to her hand.

"Hot time..." he muttered in his sleep. He flopped from one side to his back and sprawled across the entire narrow bed. His arms splayed outward while his legs cocked awkwardly to each other. He still had on his long underwear—the wool at his chest stained and covered with soot and dirt. He might have tried to get out of his pants but had pushed them only as far as his knees leaving his torso and thighs still covered in the woolen fabric. Layers of clothing bunched below his waist gave him bulbous hips like he was about to wear a Victorian hoop dress. She cringed and stifled a cry as his boots desecrated the coverlet with mud. The beautiful spread her Babcia had gifted her years earlier.

She switched out the blade from one hand to the

other, stalling for time to consider the man before her. A stranger lay before her no different than on their wedding night. Rare moments of tenderness lasted no more than the few minutes for him to be satisfied, making her toes involuntarily curl at the thought. Their time together may have been good in the beginning but now that seemed a lifetime ago.

Her thumb grazed the shaft at the intersection of the metal blade and the wooden handle. The cold steel prickled her skin in direct contrast to the heat of her palm warming the wood. She took a step into the room. A couple bare toes caught on the hem of her nightgown, causing her to trip over the threshold. She stumbled a few steps as bad as the drunken sot in the bed. Her knees stopped just short of the wooden footboard, but the razor kept going. It took flight, landing on the bedspread with a muted thump coming back to accost her senses. She held as still as the stone statue of a local Civil War veteran forever frozen in time. His blank eyes stared out over the intersection of Second and Church streets, where folks now rubbed his boots to ward off bad luck. Had she run into bad luck?

Narcisco never moved. His eyelids remained closed as if he'd entered the land of the dead. *Though I walk through the valley of death...*

The man resided in his drunkenness—passed out and snoring—oblivious to dark thoughts filling up their bedroom like a swirl of black smoke.

She righted herself and grabbed the blade with both hands as she tried to stop tremors working down her arms. Her gaze landed on the opening where he'd tried to undo as many buttons of his innerwear as possible.

Her initial plan nicked at his arms or face with the

sharp edge, but wickedness came in an instant overruling all sane thought. Years of verbal abuse brought forth a new idea. What about needling the sharp tip of the razor around his navel, push a little, and maybe draw some blood. No one need be the wiser unless he chose to tell how his wife poked a hole in his stomach. What started out as just a threat soon became a nice ripe idea of revenge to counter-balance his plans of leaving.

Narcisco snorted near as loud as Ol'Sam demanding fresh feed. Zerelda leaned backward and considered crouching down. Had he surfaced to some level of consciousness? His eyelids fluttered, and his lips moved as he mumbled, "...hot time..." He settled down and quieted his singing to a low hum.

She took a step closer to kneel down alongside the bed. Pain in her kneecap shot upward toward her hip, causing an involuntary gasp. But Narcisco still did not move. His arms continued to be splayed outward at awkward angles to his torso, but now his legs were straight, and his feet flopped so his toes pointed in opposite directions. Zerelda brought her arm up from her side to rest the weapon on his stomach, waiting for a reaction from him.

Nothing.

She fiddled the tip into one of the buttonholes catching the sharp edge on the fabric. Two bits of thread broke free but were so limp from multiple washings they didn't have the energy to stand up. Only to wilt much like their lives as a small sob caught in her throat. Zerelda hovered the blade over his exposed stomach, rustling a few dark hairs curling below his navel as light as if a summer breeze had caught them.

Narcisco groaned. Her gaze traveled up his chest past his browned neck, where scruffs of hair curled upward into a question mark then to his face. His eyelids fluttered and popped open, and the whites of his eyes shone with an unearthly glow as his pupils darted from one side of his eye sockets to the other.

"Hell, woman," he exclaimed, not bothering to look anywhere except her face as her arm floated inches above his stomach. "'Bout scared the hair off my head."

"No way you leaving me for another woman."

He lowered his gaze down her arm. His eyes widened as the moonlight glinted off the blade. Narcisco spewed spittle when he coughed in surprise. The spray in her direction felt as harsh as mud thrown from under a wagon wheel plowing through a puddle.

"W-o-m-a-n...." he slurred.

If she were a betting woman, she'd place her entire hat collection on the fact he showed equal parts *tanked-up* and scared beyond question.

His left hand came up hard and fast as he clamped onto her wrist. She tensed at his strong grip making the razor jitter up and down a couple inches above his stomach like a nervous insect. She pushed up, but he held firm. A war of muscles and strength kept the blade pointing downward. He'd feel more than a nick of his stomach if she'd let her arm go limp. Let the blade slice down. Let him suffer the consequences.

Why was he not doing more? Narcisco had the strength to fling her backward to the floor. She'd land in a broken pile of bones as his brawny muscles far outweighed her slight frame. He'd be the lion flinging a poor rabbit in the air. Maybe being so drunk slowed his brain, making him unable to process imminent danger.

Maybe he was testing her to see how far she'd carry their earlier argument.

A spasm in her arm shook over-extended muscles, and the pain screamed upward as if squeezed between the jaws of a vise. The point moved closer to Narcisco.

His arm also jerked as if her arm had connected with his to be one limb. He had but a split second to react. In that instant, he moved the wrong way, and the blade came down...hard and piercing...below his waist.

Zerelda shrieked as blood squirted up as beautiful as a fountain. It bathed her arms, chest, and face in red. She squirmed away from the bed, scooting as erratic as a spider along the floor, grabbed hold of a dresser knob, and pushed herself up to a standing position. Her stomach heaved and thrust chunks of dinner upward as waves of moonlight pinpricked her senses.

All his fault...but oh God, what had she done? She could not bear to think of it.

His screams—or hers—faded in the dark bedroom as her arms and legs gave out, and a black murkiness shut her off from reality.

****

"Ma'am, ma'am."

A voice scarce above a whisper floated over Zerelda.

"Ma'am, you be 'wake?"

Ella, Ella, are you here? Zerelda recognized the young gal's sweet timbre. *Are you beside me? Time to get ready for the ball? Are we to be late?* Zerelda tried to open her eyes to no avail. Her eyelids were glued shut. She tried to open her mouth to respond, but the taste of iron weighed heavy on her lips and tongue, making her stomach clench.

"Here," the tender voice encouraged again, "let me wash your face."

A cloth as soft as clouds covered Zerelda's face while warm liquid trickled toward her ears and neck. Another cloth, this one dry and a bit scratchy, swabbed up some rivulets heading for her shoulders. Tender fingers moved over her face while a memory as deep as love moved through her. Babcia, dear woman, caring for scraped knees and elbows.

"Babcia, are you here? Why didn't you tell me you were coming? I'd have been standing at the train station waiting."

"Ma'am, it's me, Ella. Do you not remember me?"

Ella. But I sent you away. We no longer had the money to take care of you. Oh, how I've missed you. Zerelda tried to raise up on one elbow, but parts of her body blared out in alarm. The face cloth fell away, and she pried open her eyelids but a mere slit. She turned her head side to side then her gaze landed on Ella crouched on her knees in front of Zerelda.

Sunbeams spotlighted the ugliness surrounding her except for Ella's sweet face. Zerelda focused on the young gal.

"Go slow," Ella said, placing both hands on Zerelda's shoulders to help her to a half-sitting position. "Let me help you. I think you've been in an accident."

"Accident?" Zerelda struggled to an upright position and looked away from Ella to survey the bedroom. Blood coated the spread as if an entire bucket of paint had been poured out with much of it sloshing onto her as well. A mixture of dark burgundy with crusty greenish-yellow blotches covered the front of her nightgown like a child's finger painting. A cloud of rancid odors made her nose wrinkle, and she gagged the more she tried to get away from it. "How...how did I have an accident in my own house?"

"Ma'am, you're scarin' me." Ella coughed out her words like a barking dog as the smell penetrated the room. The young gal pushed and tugged at the buttons of the soiled nightgown. "We have to get these clothes off of you."

Zerelda shook her head side to side. Her fingers shook and fumbled about with the buttons making the task near to impossible for Ella. "I...came to...bed," she stammered, as bits and pieces of last night returned, and the jigsaw puzzle of thoughts started to form a picture. "Mr. Boronza laid there on the bed snoring...and I watched...him...for a few minutes. Where is he? Has he gone to the firehouse?" She reined in the hand she pointed with, clutched it to her chest, and surveyed the bedroom, looking for someone not there.

"Oh ma'am, you alone here. I knocked and knocked. The back door swung open like it had a mind of its own. I called and called, but no one answered. Scared me fierce when I heard moaning...thought it were a ghost." Ella's shoulder shook like a chill had run through her body with those few last words. "But I called some more and at last heard you moan. And...I followed a trail of red dots from the back door to here."

"You came?"

"You know how my head works," Ella answered. "Please, ma'am. I had a nightmare this morning jes' as the sun peeked between the trees. You was goin' down under the water; you know, drowning. I hurried up, finishin' my chores for Mrs. Barnerd, and rushed o'er here faster than if I were bein' chased by a bull. You always tol' me to believe in my dreams. This time I listened to my nightmare. 'Member how you always say *dreams in the morning, heed the angel's warning?*"

Ella worked her fingers swift enough to undo most of the buttons on the nightgown while batting away Zerelda's hands as she tried to help.

Zerelda gingerly slipped the nightgown down from her shoulders in order to slide the sticky cloth past her bottom and down to her ankles in one motion. She was left clothed in knee-length pantaloons with a cotton chemise covering her chest. The fabric had become nearly see-through after being pushed across the washboard so many times. Her arms instinctively rose to cover her front as modesty surprised her in this most incredible situation.

"Are you my angel?" Zerelda's voice quivered as her body began to shake. "Have I done something wrong?" The question squirted from her lips before being able to stop. Saliva mixed with rehydrated blood from her face dribbled off her chin to the chemise. "Is Mr. Boronza here?"

"No, ma'am. I jes' said only you were here."

Zerelda moved to sit up taller as one hand brushed against something hard. She looked down to see a blade covered in dried blood. It was such a close match to the dark brown floorboards she almost didn't see it. She tried to wrap her fingers around the weapon but found it stuck to the floor, the same as how her eyes had been glued shut. Her mind began playing tricks as mental images flipped through like a hundred pictures in a book, with each one a tad changed from the last. A sharp object striking the bedspread as light sparkled off a shiny blade begging for attention. Every muscle ached; she had no memory of him striking out, but her body felt bruised as if it had been swatted across the room as effortlessly as one thwacks at an annoying mosquito.

And then nothing. Darkness, no sound, nor even passage of time. Nothing until dear Ella's voice.

Chapter Eight

October of 1907, A Trial Like No Other

"Not guilty," Judge Shields repeated, directing his stare at Attorney Cruickshank.

"Yes," the attorney confirmed.

"Sir, am I to understand you are entering a plea of this woman's innocence? Am I to assume we will be calling a jury of the woman's peers to hear this case?"

Mr. Cruickshank opened his mouth in protest of the judge's prejudices but chose to remain quiet. He looked over toward Zerelda. She'd ever-so-slightly cracked open her eyelids and gave him the most imperceptible nod ever fostered as her body remained draped over the tabletop while the escaped hat rested upside down on the floor.

The attorney grimaced in her direction even if they had gone over and over the night in question with her never wavering from her innocence. He'd pressured her to plead guilty and throw herself on the mercy of the court. But she'd resisted.

Zerelda had not committed Mayhem on her husband. She wasn't a violent person. If such a horrendous event actually occurred, though, those few moments upon waking to Ella's whispers held bits and pieces of memory she hadn't retrieved. Ella had fussed and muttered while administering to Zerelda's needs and all the while letting her come to her senses without insistence. No memory surfaced of how or why she ended up on the floor of the bedroom covered in blood. As hard as she tried, her memory remained locked.

Silence reigned.

A scrape of a boot on the wooden floor echoed loud as thunder through the hushed courtroom as spectators and participants alike waited for Mr. Cruickshank to continue. He cleared his throat and rustled a few papers on the table in front of him, as if he were giving great thought on how to proceed, and then turned his back on the judge. He continued the slow circle to survey the rows of men beginning to squirm in their hardback chairs. He smiled at a few, nodded at one or two more, then his gaze landed a few seconds longer on two women sitting toward the back of the courtroom. Ella and Corey sat side by side with their backs ramrod straight and a gorgeous hat piled high on each of their heads. Their purses had been trapped on each lap as if they were animals pressing to escape. Ella gave him a large toothy grin. He smiled a bit wider but sobered once his attention caught Corey's stern scowl.

"Sir," Mr. Cruickshank said, squaring his shoulders, then turning back to Judge Shields. "You are welcome to parade twenty, nay fifty, jurors in front of this case, and my client will still be found innocent of any and all charges."

The judge let his focus move toward Narcisco. He fidgeted on the hard seat like a man being tortured on a bed of nails. His condition proved frighteningly obvious to those already savvy of the case in front of them.

"Mr. Boronza," the judge spoke, "are you in favor of a trial by jury?"

"Your Honor," Mr. Cruickshank interrupted. The judge's eyebrows shot up. "This is unacceptable asking the petitioner's opinion before the trial has even gotten underway. Won't his time come when he's put on the witness stand?"

"You dare to question me?" the judge growled. "One more word and you'll be in contempt of this court. Tell me how your client will be served by this behavior. I'm thinking high and dry without another attorney to represent her."

Mr. Cruickshank's gasp at this kind of continued prejudice against his client sputtered to a whine by the judge's vigorous pounding of the gavel.

"Court is adjourned," the man yelled above the fray. "We will meet back here tomorrow morning promptly at ten to begin selecting a jury."

****

"Men will sit in judgment of you." Mr. Cruickshank answered Zerelda's question as soon as they were seated in a small room down the hall from the courtroom. "A couple places, such as Utah or the Wyoming territory, you will find women are allowed. But, from what I understand, seldom does a judge agree."

"But I'll be found wanting long before any evidence can be presented. Before Ella or Corey Strayer can plead my innocence." Zerelda strangled a handkerchief between both hands as she spoke.

This whole conversation caused Mr. Cruickshank's lips to pucker like he'd been sucking on a lemon. Either he didn't have the patience to continue this conversation, or the full impact of what had happened to Narcisco had now sunk in. Her attorney paused and waited for her to continue asking more. But to what purpose? He'd as much as admitted a fair trial being impossible.

"Who gets to go first?"

"I beg your pardon?"

"Who gets to tell their story first—my husband or me?"

"Mr. Boronza," her attorney said, his voice a bit muffled as he placed both hands over his face and massaged his eyes. He appeared stuck in a bad dream, yet this was her nightmare, and she'd hired him to fix her life. Mr. Cruickshank had admitted early on he'd spent little time in the courtroom and now regret for taking her case appeared etched on his face. "He's the plaintiff, so he'll tell his story first."

"Miss Strayer," Zerelda began. "She's the real reason you took my case. Am I right?"

He nodded.

"Miss Strayer mentioned you've helped her on occasion. Something about always having some trick to play on the scoundrels she encounters. Of how they come around in due time to see their own actions created the problem. You have to work your same magic now." Her heart beat so fast a ringing in her ears made the whole room reverberate like a tunnel. She tried to fill her lungs but the stagnant air smelled of old cigars. She coughed a couple of times to slow some tears threatening to fall. "I blame Narcisco. I'm here because of him. His fault…" Continuing hurt her throat. No one knew exactly what happened as her memories remained under lock and key, and Narcisco didn't seem to be forthcoming. He seemed to revel in the show more than the telling.

"I'll do the best I can, but it won't be easy," he replied, his voice rising to make it sound more like a question. Silence surrounded them for a few minutes while Zerelda dabbed at her eyes with the wrung-out handkerchief, and her attorney sat lost in thought. To her astonishment, the man unexpectedly jumped up from his chair and bumped the low table in front hard enough to scatter papers to the floor. "Lizzie Borden!"

"Excuse me?" Zerelda startled and turned as if the woman might have been standing behind her wielding an axe.

"I can argue a woman charged with a crime such as this, yes...yes...less than murder but still such a horrible crime..." Mr. Cruickshank stuttered and stammered, appearing to have lost his senses. He plopped down into a hardback chair across the room, stood again, and circled around the table. The whole time he kept raising his hands upward as if directing a choir and down toward the floor, appearing to shoo out a lazy cat. He kept muttering further words, "jury...women...peers."

"Mr. Cruickshank," she said loud enough for him to stop pacing and to focus on her. "What are you talking about?"

"Bear with me," he began, coming to a standstill in the center of the room. "Lizzie Borden killed her parents."

"Yes, I know. *Lizzie Borden took an axe and gave her mother forty whacks, and when she saw what she had done, she gave her father forty-one.* But Narcisco is still alive. I've not committed murder. Not even Mayhem, as they keep saying."

"Wait, wait, hear me out. In 1893, women were

thought to be too emotional and unstable to sit in a courtroom all day and listen to attorneys argue the law. But when Lizzie Borden went on trial, her attorney argued a jury of her peers—meaning other ladies—would understand the trials and tribulations of womenfolk. Women had not been looked at in this way before. Not saying I agree we need to put women in positions already filled by men, but this offers an interesting thought exercise."

"Were there? I mean, were there any women?"

"No," he replied, shaking his head. "Sadly, her attorney didn't have success, but the brouhaha did expedite her acquittal."

"Well," Zerelda blurted out. "There's hope. Do you think you are capable of arguing a woman needs to be on the jury? Will you?"

"I can try, but Judge Shields may not even let me get the question out. He wields his gavel like a sledgehammer."

Zerelda waited. This tact would either help her cause or create more anger.

"What evidence do you believe Mr. Boronza's attorney has?" Mr. Cruickshank settled back down into a chair and shuffled through more papers. He mumbled, "Lack of evidence. All supposition. Maybe theory or presumption. Weapon? Claim self-defense...but from a drunkard? Cruelty?"

Zerelda had become invisible to him as the man looked for something on the pages or hoped to retrieve valuable insight tucked inside his brain.

"Any woman with courage and a hatpin can defend herself," Mr. Cruickshank mumbled.

"Would that have worked?" Zerelda pondered that

thought aloud while her attorney flipped through a few more pages.

"It did in Los Angeles a few years back when a would-be daytime thief had an incensed woman charging at his face wielding a six-inch hatpin she kept tucked in her bonnet," he continued, not appearing to want or need any comment from Zerelda. "Why didn't you just use a hatpin to get his attention?"

Zerelda started to answer but could see he verbalized random thoughts under his breath and didn't need her input. The most damning evidence appeared to be her husband's condition or lack thereof of his appendage. He'd suffered a gash so deep it was irreparable yet no knife existed. She cleared her throat. Had Mr. Cruickshank come to the same conclusion?

"Harassment...not punishable by law...violence against a wife...hard to convict," he continued to mumble under his breath. "Do we take his word for the injury or make him present it as evidence? In that case, neither side has any solid proof..."

Their strategy should have long ago been determined. Before they spoke another word, Zerelda fearing her attorney had absolutely no idea what to do, a knock came at the door. Her heart sank to her empty stomach as the pounding on the door signaled an end to their meeting. And of her little bit of freedom. She'd be led back to the lockup while he'd walk out the front door of the courthouse.

Chapter Nine

October of 1907, Jury of Peers

As the jury selection began the next morning, Mr.
Navarro's name had been called to occupy a chair
opposite to and not far from Narcisco. Zerelda's
husband sat at a table with his attorney, and she feigned
a false composure after settling into the hard chair next
to Mr. Cruickshank at a matching table to the right. She
smiled at the grocer, and he, in turn, returned with a
curt nod. And then, oh what a surprise. The plaintiff's
attorney jumped up and demanded the man be excluded
from the jury.

"He knows this woman!" Mr. Walton yelled,
raising one arm more dramatic than an evangelistic
orator. To his credit, the man was quick to recognize
familiarity.

From whispers behind his back, Benjamin Walton
thought of himself also as a superior *hawkshaw*—
private investigator—taking on cases he hoped proved
to be the most sensational. Rumor had it, too, he
couldn't keep his mouth shut. Seems he had trouble
holding his reactions intact, making him a blustery
lawyer with a knack for acting. He claimed to be
talented, but his true gift looked more like a grand
imitation of a vaudevillian.

"Why else would they greet each other?" he

demanded.

"Sir," Judge Shields interrupted, "if you do not want this man on the jury, say so. You do not need to make a spectacle."

Narcisco's attorney returned to his chair at the same time Mr. Navarro climbed down from the witness stand. The grocer walked between the two tables and grazed Zerelda's shoulder with a gentle pat of concern.

"Do you see what we have to put up with? The woman is a minx! She's vexing every man entering this courtroom no different than she bewildered my client."

A tittering of comments worked through the spectators coming in ocean waves of sound. One person even clapped hands together either in glee or astonishment. A rustling of cloth, a cough here and there, and the people settled back down. Quiet came to the courtroom.

"Mr. Walton, please seat yourself and let us continue. No need to try this case until after we've seated the jury."

Mr. Cruickshank leaned close to Zerelda and whispered, "We seem to be at a bit of an advantage. If our Mr. Walton throws a tantrum with each prospective juror called for duty, we may have to ask a few ladies to show up. You keep smiling," he said, covering her hand with his and giving a bit of a squeeze. "But not too much…"

Judge Shields pounded the gavel once. "Do I need to remind you—Mr. Cruickshank and Mr. Walton—this is not a circus. We are here for a very sobering purpose, and I will not have my courtroom made as an example of how a trial can be rendered wrong. Next, please."

Soon, three men were seated on the jury. They all

bore long beards and mustaches, masking their faces up to their cheekbones, and had placed their hats in their laps in identical orientation; triplets lined up in a row. They even turned their heads in unison whenever an attorney or the judge spoke. They watched with great concentration as each prospective juror stepped forward.

Eight men had been disqualified for a variety of reasons ranging from balking about taking time away from their duties to reluctantly admitting an inability to read to voicing all women are guilty of something. So adamant she'd done the deed that a shotgun to a steel lock and hasp couldn't open their minds. There were the couple of men who claimed they knew *all about* sweet women such as Zerelda and claimed her utmost innocence. They might have been hoping to be her knight in shining armor and have her to themselves when, in fact, they were dismissed for that strong belief.

Nine more were needed before the trial had a chance to begin while exhaustion dogged her like an oxen's yoke around her neck. If weakness weren't a sin, she'd have removed her bonnet to cushion her head on the table and taken a nap right there in the courtroom.

But *no rest for the wicked or the weary* as her Babcia loved to say. The next prospective juror stepped up to the chair, turned toward the attorneys, and then scowled at the entire roomful of people before settling in for a few questions. His scowl must have meant a win for the plaintiff's lawyer as he soon took his place next to the others. Before long, only three jurors were needed, and there were no more men available.

Zerelda's mask of confidence faded, and finding enough facial muscles to keep smiling became a losing challenge.

"Sir." Mr. Walton spoke as he skittered around the table to approach the tall podium from which Judge Shields lorded down upon them, but the judge failed to halt him quick enough. "I suggest we adjourn until more can be called to serve. Do you agree?"

"Once again, Mr. Walton," the judge began, "you planning on running this show, or might you allow me the pleasure to take care of my courtroom?"

"Another point for us, I believe." Mr. Cruickshank had taken to doing a whispering commentary of the proceedings for Zerelda. Narcisco's attorney acted reckless and appeared foolish at times with his vaudevillian act overshadowing the importance of the case. But was it enough to sway the proceedings? If that happened, her husband might be the one to pay the price for these antics.

"Narcisco's attorney fancies himself rather an upstart," her attorney concluded.

She nodded at his words but fear crept up her spine.

"Mr. Walton and Mr. Cruickshank, if you please, approach the bench."

Both men made their way as comical as grade schoolers trying to walk fast without breaking into a run. The three men leaned in close, resulting in some heated whispers raging between them and words drifting through the air of *Lizzie Borden, circumstantial evidence, empathy*...on and on. Zerelda sneaked a peek to the spectators and caught sight of both Ella and Corey.

She let her gaze meander over the jury of men. They all appeared to be focusing on the discussion at the judge's bench, giving her the freedom to explore the faces of those set to determine her fate.

She felt stronger for the women seated behind her and yet more scared, knowing these men were part of the reason she lived in fear for both her life and her sanity. Thoughts of these men showing cruelty to the women in their lives wandered through her thoughts. Were any of them true gentlemen? She questioned if they were capable to view without prejudice some circumstances as unavoidable.

Mr. Cruickshank walked back to the table as a wide smile changed his face to nearly handsome. He tugged at the bottom edges of his wool vest even though his slender frame prevented any piece of clothing to ride up his torso. Another habit she found somewhat endearing.

"Judge Shields is going to request six women show up tomorrow for possible seating of the three remaining positions on the jury," he whispered, skirting the table to sit down next to her. His excitement glowed in his eyes. "This is going to make the newspaper."

As if their tale wasn't already the biggest story these small towns had seen in a very long time. The last one had been of a young farmer—hastily deputized to help hunt down a jewel thief—being shot by the suspected robber. The young fellow had died of stomach wounds while the ne'er-do-well had hobbled off into a nearby orchard—bad feet and all—jumped an old wobbly fence and reportedly boarded a train destined for Ohio. Sightings raged on for weeks of seeing a man limping while trying to hide his face as anyone approached. In the most absurd explanations, he became as mythical as a ghost by eluding capture.

Able-bodied citizens marveled at his monumental abilities to become invisible even with so much information reported about him. As soon as Zerelda and Narcisco's troubles gained attention, though, that story withered on the vine. Readers were lucky to find any news of the jewel thief, although sometimes a couple lines showed up on the last page.

But now, this next segment of the story of placing women on a jury to sit in judgment of another woman had history written all over it. Perfect timing in the early years of the 1900s as the country looked for a new passion. Mr. Cruickshank took a moment to lean back on the chair he'd claimed, hook his thumbs into the vest pocket slits, and let out a long, satisfying sigh as if he'd unexpectedly won the grand prize of a horse race. Or won the entire trial before the initial rap of the judge's gavel to start those proceedings.

And thus, the day in court ended with the banging of the gavel while participants and interested parties rose to watch the judge leave the courtroom. Attorneys shuffled and jammed papers into brown bridle leather briefcases—tightening the straps secure over secret evidence. Spectators filed out to resume their normal lives. Jurors puzzled over what tomorrow might bring, and Zerelda had to follow the sergeant-in-arms back to the little cell. Locked up for another night so as not to do further damage to man nor beast. She puzzled how her guilt in this scenario overrode her survival at the hands of a beast. She worried the jurors had made up their minds and her future sealed.

All she remembered from the night in question came at random moments in staticky glimpses of the argument she and Narcisco had before he disappeared into the darkness. Nothing within her memories helped her to know if he had left on his own accord or been helped by someone. A vacuous black hole existed where she wanted to retrieve those minutes back. Nothing until she awoke to Ella's insistence.

Zerelda stretched out on the flattened mattress laid over a rectangle frame and let weary muscles and bones be taken over by gravity. The bonnet had been holding her loose bun in place and when she removed it, her hair came cascading down long past her shoulders. It felt freeing. She placed the hat at the foot of the bed hoping to keep the fabric as clean as possible and acceptable for another day in court. After unlacing each stubborn button and sliding off well-worn ankle-high shoes, she hung her coat over the bars as a curtain from prying eyes.

Contemplating the term *circumstantial evidence* helped a bit—of course she'd be set free—as nothing gave credence to Narcisco's claims. The only proof might be the blade she'd found stuck to the floor upon waking. After forcing her jagged fingernails around the contour of the weapon, she popped it free from the floor, exposing dark brown wood outlined with the dried blood left behind. The whole time she kept her gaze on Ella. Working feverishly with her hand hidden under the cover of the discarded nightgown, she'd slid the object under the nightstand for retrieval later. Even in her confused state, clear thoughts came through how the bloodied straight razor, or knife, needed to be hidden. Yet tricks of amnesia kept rewriting her memories until she couldn't distinguish reality from insanity.

Ella's only knowledge of that distorted morning

was finding Zerelda's eyes crusted closed, a trail of red dots, and a mess to clean up. Ella knew nothing about Narcisco or his whereabouts.

And what might Narcisco remember? The rye mash had altered his perception, and his memory proved as scattered as a kid turned around in the funhouse by one too many mirrors while scary clowns popped up.

Zerelda rolled over to her left side toward the wall and let a long-needed night of sleep overtake her thoughts. Maybe she'd find her smile tomorrow.

Chapter Ten

October of 1907, Let the Performance Begin

"Your honor," Mr. Walton began with a large flourish of one arm toward Heaven.

Zerelda's attorney turned to her with a knowing smile presenting itself of how Narcisco's lawyer had to work his horse and pony show.

"I endeavor to prove Mr. Narcisco Boronza, my client, became irreparably wounded by his wife, one Mrs. Narcisco, nee Zerelda, Boronza, and how this woman"—at this point, attorney Walton gleefully turned and pointed a juddering finger toward her—"is the cause for all of my client's discomfort and stress."

"Sir..." Mr. Cruickshank tried to interrupt.

"Nay, Attorney Cruickshank, you may not speak," Mr. Walton yelled. "My client deserves a fair and equitable resolution to the dire straits his wife has put him in. Do not interrupt me nor disallow my opening statements. You will have your moment."

Mr. Cruickshank sat down after noting the judge's noncommittal attitude. Zerelda had been reassured her side of the story would be given adequate time. So, she watched and waited. Her smile masked fearful thoughts.

"Gentlemen...and er...ladies of the jury," Mr. Walton continued as three ladies had been placed alongside nine male jurors, "if you will indulge me." He swung his heaven-bound arm toward Narcisco Boronza. "Look at this man. Look closely at him, into his eyes, into his heart, and into his soul. This man has been a stalwart of the community—a family man, a successful businessman, and a volunteer within the community to make the village a better place for all of us. This is a man with friends willing—nay falling over each other—to get him back on his feet after a devastating fire at his mill. This is a man willing to help anyone asking, including a young lad seeking advice on becoming a deputy fire chief." At this point, Mr. Walton turned his gaze to a young fellow of about fifteen or sixteen who rose a finger to the brim of his hat toward the attorney. "This is a man who is willing to lie down in front of a wild horse to save your child."

"God, the man can bluster," Mr. Cruickshank whispered to Zerelda as Mr. Walton paused to take in a new lungful of hot air.

"This is a man who needs reassurance he can fall asleep in his own bed...in his own house...without wondering if he'll wake in the morning missing parts of his body," he said, with slow deliberation while he eyeballed each juror. "Let me teach you in the ways of the law. When a woman's violent actions are free of choice, she needs to be punished to the fullest extent of the law. Let me repeat. Whether it be murder, treason, or violence against her husband, if it came from her own free will, the law protects the husband."

Mr. Walton scrubbed his hand over his clean-shaven face. Not a sound. He clamped both hands down to the railing separating himself from the jurors. Their complete attention focused on him, with one person looking away as he stared from one to the next.

"This is a man needing your judgment to rain down on his wife, securing her in a prison where she will no longer harm another," he concluded.

Any sound in the courtroom simmered down as a flame is reduced to glowing embers. No one dared to move, to whisper, or to let the next moment go unheard, determining someone's fate. Mr. Cruickshank pushed back his chair, cleared his throat, stomped a bit heavier than usual around the table, and came to a standstill in front of the jury of nine men and three women. A full minute passed as the attorney collected his thoughts and let his opponent's words fade.

"Ah well....ah. So, you've heard my esteemed colleague's opening statement. Now, will you please listen to the correct side as the story unfolds? My client," Zerelda's attorney turned away from the jury and smiled at her, "is innocent."

He let his words hover in the air. Mr. Walton hadn't claimed the exact word of *guilt* as he blathered on and on about the plaintiff's qualities. Mr. Cruickshank waited while his comment floated throughout the room, hoping it would gain credence.

"She may have made a couple of mistakes," he continued. "Who in this courtroom is free from sin?" He paused while a few spectators nodded. "With all due respect, my colleague spoke of intent but let's look at the law from a different angle. How much can one person endure before that point of breaking? The presumption of the law speaks to a person being innocent above guilt, and that, if a woman acts by the command and coercion of her husband to commit an act against her will, she may not be punished."

Mr. Cruickshank wandered around the courtroom with his hands clasped behind his back. He acted like it was a stroll in the park. "Innocent before guilty," he repeated.

"But let's examine what we know so far. Zerelda, our Mrs. Boronza, is a kind and gentle woman not prone to anger or wild outbursts. She creates beautiful bonnets, as exhibited by the one she wears today. She has maintained a house and home for her husband of many years, and I must say without prior incidences such as this. She and Mr. Boronza have enjoyed the fruits of his labors as well as the curse of decline. She has lived with never a sour comment to anyone or from anyone in the village. This is a woman of upstanding quality, education, and manners. And yes, although she may not be perfect, do we condemn a woman for the sole act of defending herself? Consider how you might react after a constant barrage of insults, condemnation, and criticism all curiously wrapped up in the threat of desertion."

Mr. Cruickshank paused and then turned toward his client with exaggerated slowness. He swept his gaze over toward the plaintiff and his attorney. The judge was his next target. But Judge Shields stared at a spot beyond them all with great concentration as if to open a portal to happier times. Mr. Cruickshank's gaze landed back on the spectators who were entranced by his sing-song voice and gentle, soothing words. Zerelda loved how he had everyone in the palm of his hand until...

"Your honor," Mr. Walton crudely interrupted the moment, "let's get to the good part of how she ran. Or, should I say, pedaled away."

****

"My name is Ella."

"Do you have a last name, Ella?" Mr. Walton inquired with less drama than his opening statements. Kid-glove treatment, working an angle to get his desired results.

"Aw, Ella, be fine. But, if it be important, Mrs. Barnerd will give me her last name."

"All right, Ella, can you tell us what happened the morning you found Mrs. Boronza."

"Do I have to?"

"Yes. We need to know why you were there, what you found, and how you helped your former employer."

"Aw, Mrs. Boronza," Ella mumbled, bowing her head. She looked over toward Zerelda with a deep sadness in her dark brown eyes. "I don't want to say anything to hurt her."

"Please, we only seek the truth. That is all." Mr. Walton nudged Ella as tender as a butterfly in the palm of his hand moments before squishing her.

Zerelda glanced over to her attorney, noting his downturned lips and scowl pulling his brows together.

"Truth be told, Mrs. Boronza is the best person I've ever known. I so loved helpin' her all those years 'til they couldn't afford me no longer. I'd 'ave almost done her work for nothin' 'cept I'm always helpin' my ma and now Mrs. Barnerd. Brings in a little money to help where I can…"

"No…no," Mr. Walton tried to interrupt, "we need to know about the morning in question. Nothing else."

Zerelda's attorney concentrated on scratching a couple notes on the journal he had in front of him. He must have recognized a subject to pursue once given the chance to question the young gal.

"Well," Ella replied. "If'n you don't want to know anything else, how you gonna get to the truth?"

Snickers resounded throughout the courtroom. Judge Shields thumped his gavel on the wooden block. The *thwack*, lackluster from over-spent enthusiasm, had no firmness, but at least the roomful of people quieted down.

"Attorney Walton," the judge said as his shoulders slumped a bit. "May I ask why you are questioning this girl. Seems to me the defendant is more likely to have her on the stand than you."

"Your Honor, I believe my questions will bring forth the real story from her."

Judge Shields waved off any further comment.

"So," the attorney said, turning on his heels back to Ella. "Please continue."

"I had a nightmare."

"A nightmare," he stated. A puzzled look creased his face giving Zerelda the impression the attorney for Narcisco had become unsure of the direction this questioning could take.

"Yessir," she replied. "Don't tell me you ain't never had one of those. Truth always lies close below the surface. We be told fairy tales in our dreams, but nightmares make sure we sit up and take notice."

"All right," the attorney said, clearing his throat. "Tell us of your nightmare."

"Well, to be sure, I had two nightmares. But the first one don't truly matter less'n you hook it up with the second one."

"All right," Mr. Walton sighed. "So please tell us the first."

"My mama always said dreaming of mice tells us

family problems be on the horizon."

"And?"

"I fell back asleep pretty quick 'cuz we all got problems, ain't we? Didn't mean much to me." Ella looked toward the attorney questioning her as if she needed confirmation. He didn't say anything this time. "Then another nightmare happened right on top of the first one."

Mr. Walton had the look of a man weary from walking a hundred miles. He sat down and waved a hand for her to continue.

"I woke up scared. And I knew without a doubt her guardian angel was muddlin' with me, and both dreams were about Mrs. Boronza. I got scared enough Mrs. Barnerd could've chained me to a post an' I'd gotten away. I'd have done all my chores in two hours even if she'd piled a day's worth on top of me. I knew gettin' to Mrs. Boronza more important than anythin' else might happen that day."

"Can you tell me why?"

"I dreamt of red dots."

"Red dots." He stood up so fast papers rousted on the table enough to take temporary flight.

"Do ya need me to talk louder?"

"No. I only want to make sure we all fully understand."

"Yes," Ella reiterated. "Red dots splattered all over my mind, and I jes' knew Mrs. Boronza be in trouble. Can't always explain things, but I went there."

"What did you find?"

"Nothing."

"Nothing? What about red dots? What about Mrs. Boronza? Or even the master of the house—was he there?"

"Oh, he weren't there."

"But you found her. And what about the red dots?"

"Yes."

"Yes? Please explain."

Ella paused, her eyes expanding as if she were seeing the red dots anew. "I followed 'em."

"You followed what?"

"The red dots. Well, actually, they were brown dots in the dry dirt by the back door. I went inside 'cuz the back door weren't latched. I called, but no one answered. But I saw more dots. Red all across the kitchen floor toward the bedroom."

"So you followed those dots. What did you find?"

"Poor ma'am. She laid there all sprawled on the floor of the bedroom, flat on her back, blood covering near the whole front of her, and her face lookin' like she wore a red mask. After helpin' to wash her eyes, nose, and mouth, I helped her up. It took her a long time before she spoke to me, then we tried to figure out what had happened."

"Did you?"

"Did I what?"

"Figure out why you found Mrs. Boronza covered in blood," Mr. Walton demanded. His full-of-frustration voice rang a bit louder than necessary in the courtroom. He'd been defeated of his bluster just trying to keep Ella's testimony on track. "Weren't you alarmed?"

"Might 'ave been," Ella responded. "But her bein' alive and all right and Mr. Boronza nowhere to be found made us safe."

"Let me ask this another way...weren't you scared you found your former employer covered in dried blood and the man of the house missing?"

"Oh, I suppose a bit but Mrs. Boronza tol' me not to worry."

"And you believed her."

"'Course," Ella replied. Her voice held the innocence of spoken truth. "Never had no reason to think otherwise."

Mr. Walton shook his head back and forth to give himself a couple seconds to collect his thoughts against a woman clearly without guile or guilt. Her belief in her former employer of having done nothing wrong clearly disrupted his plan.

"Please tell the court what happened next."

"Well...we traced the red dots back to the kitchen door from where I come a while earlier."

"Correct me if I'm wrong. The red dots in your dream were blood. Can you explain why you thought they were blood?"

"Such a beautiful trail. Kind of like bread crumbs but so much brighter."

"And?"

"Mr. Walton, you seem awful impatient." Ella spoke with authority yet bent her head forward in supplication for fear of being reprimanded. "Sure as I'm sittin' here, I got a story, but there ain't no reason to hurry the tellin' before the right time."

"Go on," he responded. His exasperation showed in shifting his weight from one leg to the other.

"Well, we retraced the dots. Didn't see any sign of Mr. Boronza but the missus stayed pretty shook up."

"Did you find anything else when you were retracing your steps?"

"Yessir."

"Something you've never seen?"

"Never one of those in all my days."

"But you knew what it might be."

"I guessed. Been around 'nough animals to be pretty sure what I be lookin' at."

"Please give us your first thoughts when you saw it."

Ella paused, and she screwed up her face sorrier than smelling rotten eggs left too long in the larder.

"Let me ask another way. Did you do anything with it? Did you pick it up?" The attorney tiptoed through a delicate subject amongst the ladies and gents in the courtroom but knew full well he had to travel this route.

"I picked up the darn thing. It weren't no bigger'n a pork roll for breakfast..."

"You held the object? In the palm of your hand?"

"No sir. I grabbed a towel so's I couldn't see that ugly thing before pickin' up the whole bloody mess. All I could think of was tossin' it out with yesterday's trash."

"You threw it and the towel somewhere?"

"Oh yeah. Right out the window o'er the wash sink. That were the one broken a while back the day the mill burned. Shook out the ol'kitchen towel I'd wrapped it up in. Couldn't throw away the towel as that were more important than savin' the..." Ella paused. A slight blush creased her cheeks as she made it abundantly clear a word couldn't be given to the appendage in its unnatural state of detachment. "Might have taken flight for all I cared. But I saved the towel."

"But no flight occurred, am I right?"

"No. I'm pretty sure it landed in the grass jes'

87

below the window."

"What do you suppose happened next?"

"Pretty sure rats enjoyed a bit of a surprise on they's tongues."

"Your Honor," Mr. Cruickshank yelled. He jumped to his feet faster than a toad avoiding a scythe. "I need to object?" His voice rose into the form of a question.

The judge raised his bushy eyebrows. "On what basis?"

"Sir, I find this graphic testimony highly uncomfortable for the ladies on the jury. Do you not?"

"Overruled. Weren't you the one wanting women to be seated?"

"I'd like to have my witness clarify what she is referring to," Attorney Walton chimed into the discussion. "I don't want any confusion of what she tossed might have been nothing more than a piece of rotten meat dropped on the floor the night before. The jury needs to know."

"Oh no, youse Honor," Ella piped up, wrapped up in the moment of telling her story. "Weren't rotten meat. It were what'd been cut off the master. Limp as a dead fish, kind of gray if you ask me, and something maybe them old crows might've enjoyed more'n the rats."

Fear flittered across her face. Her expression finished telling a tale full of guilt to the jury. She'd painted a picture to the opposing attorney and Judge Shields of how Zerelda could have sliced off Narcisco's penis and left the appendage lying on the floor crueler than yesterday's meat. Worse than rotten meat.

Spectators erupted with hoots and laughter as they shot surprised and curious looks toward the victim. The word sinking in to everyone's consciousness exactly what had gone missing. A man's most treasured part of his anatomy. His *cutlass,* his *best-of-three legs,* his penis hadn't only been stabbed but completely sliced off. Narcisco squirmed worse than before.

Judge Shields found strength in his wrist to bang the gavel loud enough to thunder above the ruckus.

****

Ten minutes had passed with the judge trying to quiet those in the room and to get his own composure back to some semblance of order. Judge Shields' bloated face had turned an unnatural shade of reddish-purple tighter than a balloon soon to burst. The ladies on the jury had handkerchiefs covering their mouths as if to avoid any unpleasantness from surfacing while their eyes spread open wide as saucers. One looked near to fainting as her face turned an eerie shade of olive-gray. The men seated alongside the women squirmed, adjusting and re-adjusting their clothing. They couldn't be more obvious than if they'd pulled down their pants to inspect each other. But to their credit, none of them looked toward one another nor the women seated close to them.

"Can you continue, Ella?"

Narcisco's attorney showed compassion for his witness. Did he feel guilty for taking the questioning too far? Zerelda found his reaction a curiosity. So far, Mr. Walton had exhibited care for himself and no other. She wondered if he had more questions but chose not to ask since the graphic imagery had been documented by the court recorder.

"May I ask what happened next?" Mr. Walton asked as he turned the questioning in a different direction.

"Mrs. Boronza left."

"She left." The attorney pondered her answer with those two words, rubbed at his chin as if in deep thought, and silently suggested how leaving piled on top of all the other bad choices made. He played his role to perfection. "She left; walked away? Went to the barn? Someone came for her?"

"By way of a bicycle. I helped her dress up in Mr. Boronza's clothes—even if they hung on her like a sorry ol'scarecrow—and she stole a bike from behind one of the stores."

"Stole. Let me get this right. We can add stealing to all of the other charges. Mmmm. Please continue."

"Said she wanted to go ridin' out of town."

"To where?"

"I don't know. I got left at the back door watchin' her peddle that bike faster than the Devil could chase her through the back alley and me wishin' everythin' to go back to the old ways. But guess we cain't. You tellin' me we're here for the same reason no one believes her, right?"

"Yes, Ella. We're here to find out the truth."

No one moved in the courtroom. Any sounds were deadened like going into deep water. Yet a feeling of something ready to burst like a huge cloud overhead made the silence vacuous. Like the air had been sucked out of the room. The crowd poised stiffer than a hundred mimes waiting to come alive. Waiting for someone to speak.

"Guess the truth is comin' out. I did wrong. I helped Mrs. Boronza get free." Ella broke the silence.

"Maybe not," the plaintiff's attorney muttered as

he returned to his seat. But, in mid-pose heading toward the chair, he straightened back up as if he'd forgotten his manners. "Thank you, Ella, you've been most helpful."

"You may step down, Miss Ella." The judge looked even more uncomfortable than when the charge was first read aloud. He looked over to Mr. Walton, curled his lips into a sneer as if he was scanning a field for a snake in the grass, and asked, "Do you have more witnesses?"

The attorney nodded. He ramped up his actions with a smile of pure glee as if he was going in for the kill. "And now, if it pleases the court, I'd like to call Miss Corey Strayer to the stand."

Chapter Eleven

October of 1907, Strength in Secrets

"S...o...r...r...y..."

The whispered word wormed to Zerelda's ears and she raised her gaze to meet her friend's mournful look. Ella had tried so hard to deflect Mr. Walton's questions but the *hawkshaw* had an animalistic vengeance. No denying his strength in being predatory. Mr. Cruickshank had warned Zerelda of how Ella could be an asset for the opposing attorney. That maybe they would have considered her a hostile witness if she refused to answer questions. The problem they hadn't foreseen was Ella didn't refuse. She answered each question with honesty and a lack of guile found in few. Made her a target the attorney zeroed in on without hesitation.

As Ella stepped down from the witness stand, paused as indecision mapped her face with a downturned gaze, and stretched her full lips to a thin line to say nothing more out loud. She shuffled within inches of Zerelda mouthing *s...o...r...r...y*. Zerelda felt as miserable getting Ella involved as the young gal appeared distraught in her recounting the events. Zerelda said a silent prayer nothing came up about the blood-splattered nightgown, which had now gone missing. Admission of disposing of incriminating evidence never came up. Damning if ever discovered.

The members of the jury followed Ella's progress back to the spectator area while some continued to look upset by the revelations. Others looked as if they were hoping the next witness might offer up more gratuitous titillation. Zerelda tendered her friend a weak smile in hopes she'd understand.

"Miss Corey Strayer," the bailiff spoke and then called out louder, "Miss Corey Strayer. If you'd please take the witness stand."

With deliberate caution and slow-motion action, the private investigator Zerelda had hired months earlier rose from one of the chairs reserved specifically for witnesses. The woman smoothed down her slacks, tugged on the jacket she wore, tenderly adjusted the bonnet even if it wasn't necessary, strolled down the aisle, and stepped past the low-slung gate separating the spectators from the participants, and stopped in front of the witness stand. She turned, gazed at the crowd before her, glared at the opposing attorney, plopped down on the chair awaiting her, and folded her hands in her lap.

"Your name, occupation, date of birth, and residency, please."

"Corey Strayer, Private Investigator, September 17, 1870, Lansing, Michigan."

"Are you currently employed by one Mrs. Narcisco Boronza, nee Zerelda Boronza?"

"I am."

"May I ask the purpose of that employment."

Oh, what a cocky attorney this Mr. Benjamin Walton acted near as slick as the plaintiff himself. The man even smoothed back a lock of wayward hair at almost the exact moment Narcisco Boronza did; the pomade sticky enough to hold both locks in place. Zerelda had confidence that Corey could shred them as fine as cotton thread made ready for weaving into a blanket. But for now, she watched the show before her.

"Why did Mrs. Boronza employ you?" Attorney Walton pressed Corey by repeating the question.

"Client privacy privilege if you must be reminded."

"Ah yes, of course, you don't need to answer, but you seem to be the type wanting to move these proceedings along at a clippingly fast pace. Or do you want to be considered here against your will?"

"I believe I am. As you know, being a lawyer as you call yourself, I am not inclined to answer questions that may implicate a client in any wrong-doing," she responded, then added with exaggerated emphasis, "*sir.*"

Judge Shields turned his gaze toward Corey with a look of imploring one to cooperate. Her reputation may have preceded her, and did the judge fear what else might come to light in this case? Or was it merely a lunch appointment? Maybe Mr. Walton's questioning tactics had run their useful course.

"I suppose you want to hear she came to my office for the express purpose of asking my opinion," Corey answered. A deliberate slowness on her part taunted Narcisco's lawyer.

"On what?"

"Well, let me think." She subtly tapped her right temple as if in deep thought. "We talked of men; their actions, their motivations, and how they might bend the normal everyday honest forms of living to their own benefit."

"She didn't ask you to follow her husband?"

"Might have come into the conversation," Miss Strayer hedged. Her expression was unreadable as she gazed over at the attorney. "May I ask you a question?"

"Highly unusual," he replied but acquiesced with a nod of his head. "You may."

"Have you ever thought of straying from your family?"

Mr. Walton's hand went up to his collar where his fingers struggled to find the knot for his bowtie. He fingered the fabric as if a noose had been tightened around his neck. He stared straight at the tall, imposing woman in the witness stand and paused. Once again, his face gave away his change of tactic to get answers to further his client's cause.

"Miss Strayer," he continued. "Did you or did you not pose as a salesperson looking to open a dry goods store in Cedartown? And if so, may I ask for what purpose."

"I did but found the village lacking in my needs. I lingered for a couple of weeks but never saw the potential for customers."

"You are telling me you weren't spying."

"Spying?" she questioned. "Spying on possible customers? How might snooping help me in opening a storefront if future customers thought of me as a suspicious and nosy person?"

"No...no," Mr. Walton stuttered. His face flamed to a bright red, and he looked toward the judge almost as if he wanted to object against his own witness. "No...no. Were you spying on someone while you posed as a salesperson?"

"Sounds like too much to do during one day, don't you think?"

"I don't think," the attorney shot back, then paused as he must have realized how inane his own answer sounded. He waited, took a deep breath, and appeared to collect his thoughts. After a moment, "I do question your motives."

"Well...Mr. Walton...you might want to question what kind of person you think you are, I am, and Mrs. Boronza is. I believe you to be an overbearing, insensitive, get-money-however-you-can sleazy attorney and purported *hawkshaw*; me as an upstanding first-rate woman private investigator; and Zerelda— Mrs. Boronza—as an innocent victim in your witch hunt. And I find your motives as unscrupulous. Tell me what you are hoping to find."

"The truth."

"You are looking for the truth, you say. I have nothing more to add as revealing the truth is a concept you don't appear to understand." With those few words, Miss Corey Strayer stood, smoothed her slacks where there were no creases, stood up straight and tall, pushed on the bonnet adorning her head, and stepped down from the witness stand. She turned toward Narcisco and strolled within an arm's reach of him. Contempt creased her face.

Silence descended on the courtroom once again and minutes ticked by until Judge Shields tapped the gavel on the block of wood as if he were encouraging a little doggie to move along. No enthusiasm whatsoever.

"Mr. Walton," he started, a resigned sigh escaping his lips, "do you have any other witnesses you'd care to call to the stand?"

"I do, your Honor," he replied. "I call Josef James to the stand."

A buzz the strength of bumblebees closing in on bright sunflowers resounded through the courtroom. Heads turned side to side as most were spurred by curiosity of who this Josef James might be. They were rewarded in quick order when a young man—the one who had acknowledged attention given him during Mr. Walton's opening statement—rose and walked to the witness stand keeping his eyes trained on the floor the entire way.

"Please state your name, occupation, birthdate, and residency."

"Josef James, fireman, January 15, 1890, Cedartown, Michigan."

"You are telling me your age is seventeen, correct?"

"Yes."

"Your schooling?"

"Made it through the sixth grade," Josef said. He sat up a bit taller as a smile creased his face showing pride in his accomplishment. "Ma said I could quit if I made it that far."

"And you work at the firehouse."

"Yes."

"Please tell me if you have ever met or come in contact with the woman, Miss Corey Strayer, who testified before you."

"Yes."

"Can you elaborate?"

"Can I what?"

"Can you elaborate—tell me a bit more about meeting her."

"Oh yeah, right. She came in looking for the chief...Mr. Boronza...but he weren't there when she arrived. He showed up a couple minutes later, but she left real quick-like. Maybe she hadn't wanted to meet him, but jes' there to ask questions."

"Thank you."

"Oh no, there's more."

"No, thank you. We're done here," Mr. Walton interrupted. "Please step down."

"But…"

"Your Honor, please tell the witness we are finished."

Mr. Cruickshank leaned into Zerelda and whispered, "What do you suppose he wanted to say Walton doesn't want to get out?"

Zerelda shrugged her shoulders for lack of a reason to whisper back. Her mind kept playing tricks; sometimes, she sat in this courtroom paying close attention while other times it wandered backward. Horrible moments had happened. None made any sense, such as the mill catching on fire and her husband placing blame on her. Questions continued about why did the bucket brigade work longer than usual to make sure not a single spark glowed even when a storm showered down on the village. Then with the firemen so involved in helping him rebuild the structure while giving assurances of customers returning. Josef James might know more than Mr. Walton cared to have exposed, while Zerelda hoped her own attorney showed ruthlessness in unearthing the truth.

Mr. Walton swatted his hand in dismissal of the witness, and Mr. Cruickshank didn't object nor appear to have questions to ask.

Josef removed himself from the witness stand and walked past Zerelda, giving her a lingering nod that spoke volumes to her. He proceeded straight out of the courtroom. He'd be back, though, if Mr. Cruickshank had anything to say over the proceedings. Zerelda hoped all would work in her favor.

"I have one more witness, your Honor," Mr. Walton requested.

"Sir, the day has dragged on and is growing late. Do you have many more questions?"

"One, sir."

"All right, call your witness."

"I call grocer Mr. Navarro of Cedartown."

Zerelda's heart dropped to her stomach heavier than a musket ball. She'd been so pleased when he'd been refused as a juror, never imagining he'd end up a witness to the plaintiff.

"Please state your name, occupation, birthdate, and hometown," the attorney requested once the burly man sat down.

"George Navarro, grocer, December 7, 1868, Cedartown, Michigan, and before that of Germany. I arrived a few years ago to set up a meat market. I am a law-abiding—"

"Yes, yes, I'm sure you are," Mr. Walton interrupted. "I have only one question and then I beg we adjourn until tomorrow."

The day's proceedings had become long and drawn out, the spectators were getting restless, body heat had risen ceiling-ward and suffocating to those it hovered over, and stomachs were growling for the evening meal. Mr. Navarro narrowed his gaze at the attorney, but nothing stopped the question from being asked.

"Have you ever sold the defendant, one Mrs. Narcisco Boronza—nee Zerelda Boronza—a knife?"

"Your Honor," Mr. Cruickshank yelled. His voice rose above the clamoring crowd as he stood up so fast the table moved a good six inches forward. The ensuing din prevented Mr. Navarro from answering the question right away, but he did nod his head.

Attorney Walton raised his arms in question, acting like an innocent six-year-old of any trickery. Judge Shields pounded the gavel while Mr. Navarro directed another grimacing nod toward Zerelda before directing his sad eyes toward the floor.

Mr. Cruickshank had risen to his full height. He'd shot an unmistakable sneer of contempt at his opponent after turning to stand face-to-face with the attorney as if readying for a duel. He then turned to the judge and continued in a loud voice. "We cannot adjourn. You must allow me to cross-examine the witness our esteemed colleague has already questioned. Or at least allow Mr. Navarro to give an answer, not just a nod. We cannot adjourn for the day. Our esteemed jurors are being allowed to mull this over for twelve hours with no way of knowing what that nod meant."

The judge targeted his scowl at both attorneys. He looked from one to the other, causing him to miss the block of wood protecting the desktop from the gavel. Silence reigned as a couple splinters of wood flew upward toward the judge's face following the loud hollow knock.

"Sit down, both of you," he demanded, grabbing the largest splinter after it had landed in front of him. He directed the piece of wood as a pointer, first at Zerelda's attorney then at Narcisco's lawyer. "Neither one of you will tell me how to run my courtroom. The hour is late. Mr. Navarro will be directed to answer the question tomorrow. We will take the night to recess, and I will inform each and every one of you how we will proceed when we reconvene."

Chapter Twelve

October of 1907, Countless Questions

"You may call to cross-examine," Judge Shields spoke the next morning once everyone had been seated. Strange to say, he directed his words at Zerelda instead of her attorney. The man appeared weary-eyed as if he hadn't slept one wink last night. His shoulders slumped forward as defeat defined in how he looked out over the courtroom. "I will instruct you on when the grocer will be returned to the witness stand. Cross-examine who you wish but do not linger."

"I'd like to call Ella back to the stand for cross-examination," Mr. Cruickshank replied. The man looked refreshed and ready for battle and not a bit surprised at the judge's decision. Most realized the judge did not have control to restrict witnesses, but he seemed the type to create other roadblocks.

The young gal carried herself bent over and bowed with the weight of her earlier testimony on her shoulders. She made her way from the back of the room to climb the couple of steps up to the witness stand.

"Please remember you are still under oath."

Ella responded with a faint nod of her head toward the judge, all the while keeping her eyes trained on Zerelda's attorney.

"Are you nervous, Miss Ella?"

She nodded so hard her curls bounced outward like branches in a strong wind.

"Ella, you need to answer and not merely move your head." He spoke in a kind yet stern voice. "You see those two men over there in the corner? They are busy writing down what is said. If you don't speak, we will not know how you answered."

"Yessir. But I'm scared," she responded to his original question as she slowly raised her hand to point a finger toward Mr. Walton. "This here attorney o'er there asked me questions but didn't let me answer."

"Can you tell us what you wanted the court to hear?"

"Yessir," she began. "Mrs. Boronza tol' me somethin' once she woke up."

"She told you something?"

"Nothing."

"She told you nothing?"

"No, she tol' me she don't remember nothing from the night or up 'til I woke her as she laid there on the bedroom floor."

"I don't understand," Mr. Cruickshank said.

Ella shook her head again and looked over at the two court recorders with an apology creased across her face. She shrugged and smiled.

"In my way of thinkin', if someone can't remember anythin' about why they's lying on a floor or covered up with blood or how long they been there, they's be the victim too. Somethin' done so bad they's memory threw those thoughts far away."

Mr. Walton began to object but sat back down as if he'd thought of something more useful for later.

"I know," Ella continued but stopped.

"You know what?" Mr. Cruickshank was keeping his gaze directly on her, so when she looked up, it would be his encouraging smile she'd see.

Ella pulled a handkerchief from a cuff of a long sleeve of the simple brown wool dress to wipe her nose. She took her time tucking it away once finished. "I know 'cause I can't remember certain things done to me when I were a young'un. But I weren't no criminal like you all are accusin' Mrs. Boronza of doin'."

"I object," Mr. Walton said, this time raising both arms toward the judge instead of standing up. "Can this woman tell us she is an expert in the field of the human brain? How she places herself on the same level as the German doctor Wilhelm Wundt who a mere twenty years ago began studying the field of memory and emotions? Her schooling rivals…"

"Mr. Walton," Judge Shields sighed in exasperation. "Do you want to object, or am I to assume you're trying to show us how smart you are throwing around names no one's ever heard?"

"If it pleases the court, I am asking you to consider how this small slip of a girl doesn't have the intelligence to diagnose another person's brain."

"Now I object," Mr. Cruickshank called out. "Is this witness being placed on trial by Attorney Walton or do we want to hear her testimony?"

The judge raised one hand up to silence any more objections, and a long pause followed, punctuated by a nervous cough or shuffling of feet as some of the spectators repositioned themselves. As he pondered his response, he cleared his throat. "Mr. Cruickshank, please finish your cross-examination," he declared as he glowered at the other attorney, "and let's not have any more speeches until the conclusion of the evidence."

"Can you continue Ella?"

"Yessir. I jes' want to say a person only survives in this earthly world if'n we can forget some of the bad done to us. I found ma'am lying by herself covered in blood, and I thought she were dead. But she's here being accused of hurting someone who's been downright mean to her at times. And oh boy, I have lots of stories 'bout how he ..."

"Thank you, Ella," Mr. Cruickshank stopped her from saying more.

He and Zerelda had spoken at great length about Narcisco's temper, and she knew this wasn't how her attorney wanted the verbal abuse to come to light. Hopefully, the opposing attorney didn't pick up any cues and would let this testimony slide.

"I wish to recall Corey Strayer to the stand if it pleases the court," her attorney said after Ella had stepped to the back of the room.

The private investigator rose as statuesque as ever, marched to the witness stand, turned, smoothed down her coat, and sat.

"Miss Strayer," the attorney began. "I have one question for you, and please feel free to elaborate as much as you feel is necessary. Do you know or have you had dealings with Attorney Walton before your testimony in this trial?"

"Strange you ask such a question," she commented. "As I am still under oath, I will say yes, I have had dealings with Mr. Benjamin Walton."

"Elaborate if you so please. I'd like to have it cleared up why you chose to not answer some questions earlier."

"I do not care to go into many details, but to reiterate, Mr. Narcisco Boronza has chosen poorly in the man he has hired to represent himself. I will say this attorney, though"—and here is where she pointed a finger at her target—"proved to be an excellent subject of one of my very own investigations and gave credence to the very reason we private investigators exist. He is not to be trusted. All present beware of his stealthy tricks and turns of phrase and never assume he will be faithful to whatever someone else's cause may be. He looks out for himself at all cost, no one else, and would as soon push a hostile witness in front of a horse and wagon than figure out the truth."

With *truth* being her final word, as before, Corey Strayer rose from the chair before being dismissed and walked back to her spectator chair.

Zerelda worked to suppress a smile at how one woman said so much yet divulged nothing. Mr. Walton's reputation may be in jeopardy, and he no doubt now wished he'd thought through his witness list with more care. She glanced across the two tables to spot her husband questioning his attorney with the rise of his bushy eyebrows. Mr. Walton had slunk down in the chair, avoiding any need to respond or object.

"Mr. Cruickshank, do you wish to recall any other witnesses for the plaintiff?"

"Yes, only two more before preparing for our defense. First, I'd like to recall Josef James to the stand and, after him, Mr. George Navarro."

Once the young man settled into the witness chair, the attorney had one question, which produced mixed results. He'd asked for clarification of why the opposing attorney prevented him from continuing earlier. Josef gave a slight shrug of the shoulders—and then a quick look over at the court recorders—before muttering a noncommittal statement of allegiance between firemen. No mention of loyalty to whom, whether loyalty to the plaintiff deserved favoritism, or to the revered bond within the fire department, or to their performance while fighting the mill building engulfed in flames. Mr. Cruickshank gave up, clearly getting nowhere. The young man may have been coached overnight.

Cruickshank gave up and asked the judge to recall Mr. George Navarro to the witness stand.

"Sir," the attorney greeted the grocer after he had settled in. "I believe your answer to Mr. Walton's question of if you've ever sold a knife to Mrs. Boronza did not get recorded by our two esteemed court recorders. Please give your answer to the question." Mr. Cruickshank paused, shuffled a couple pieces of paper on the table, and cleared his throat. He read out loud from one of the pages, *"Have you ever sold the defendant, one Mrs. Narcisco Boronza—nee Zerelda Boronza—a knife?"*

Spectators and participants alike leaned forward in their seats as if moving an inch closer to Mr. Navarro might speed up his answer. Mr. Navarro played the moment as a true German—solemn, stubborn to be pushed into anything unnecessary, ready to argue if need be, and all with a bit of dry humor. He cleared his throat while scowling down at Mr. Walton until the attorney found a piece of lint on his jacket to remove.

The grocer smiled as if he'd remembered a pleasant moment or conversation with the defendant. "No," he replied. A short laugh escaped from him. "I have never sold a knife to Mrs. Boronza, although I have to admit Mr. Boronza may be one of my best customers."

With that answer, Mr. Cruickshank sat down.

****

"Your Honor," Mr. Walton began while rising from the chair he'd occupied and buttoned his dress coat with slow deliberation.

Judge Shields looked upward as if answers were tucked into the stamped-tin patterns of the ceiling. He took his own sweet time before looking at the attorney and giving a pert nod to continue when no other choice presented itself.

"I know this might be highly unusual, but I request the opportunity to question my client, Mr. Narcisco Boronza, on the stand and under oath. I believe all will become clear once he is seated." Attorney Walton grinned with the smugness of a cat having caught the prize bird and didn't have to share. "Your Honor?"

The judge flicked his hand in annoyance and nodded. More a gesture of resignation than acceptance, but the attorney took it as a signal to continue and looked toward his client. Narcisco rose with great care. He pulled at his slacks to loosen them from his legs and then moved toward the steps up to the chair. One step, one foot, a second foot up in line with the first. He repeated his progress twice more and turned to sit down. Sweat had gathered on his reddened face as if even the slightest movement pushed a fiery poker into parts of his body.

"Are you all right?" Mr. Walton's solicitous attitude toward his client pointed to practiced acting skills far outweighing all else and maybe even the truth.

"Can you answer a couple of questions?"

Narcisco nodded while he slipped something from his coat pocket. A soiled handkerchief covered the item and he handled the package with great reverence to present it to the attorney as a gift.

"May I ask what you are holding?"

"Evidence," Narcisco stated with satisfaction filling his voice. The only thing missing was a trumpet fanfare to celebrate his performance.

"But sir," the attorney began, matching his client's same incredulous act. He played the part of a puzzled skunk losing sight of his next victim. "I've been under the impression no evidence existed."

Mr. Cruickshank jumped up from his chair to interrupt the proceedings, "Your Honor, how can the witness be holding evidence such as I have not been made aware of? Even his attorney *acts* surprised! This is most irregular, and I object with all due respect."

"Well, sir," the judge interjected. "You can object all you want, but I am going to allow his attorney to follow this line of questioning. Continue, Mr. Walton."

"Thank you. May I ask what you are holding, Mr. Boronza."

Narcisco began pulling back the edges of the handkerchief while the item rested in the palm of his hand. By the time the second corner had been released, the glint of a blade caught sunlight from one of the eastern windows. He held a knife in his hand.

"*The* knife," Narcisco answered. "This is the weapon used to inflict an injury on me so horrendous I will never recover."

Attorney Cruickshank's face colored the same purplish-red as the judge's the day earlier. Anger had taken on a bright color as he sputtered all during the time Zerelda kept pulling on his jacket sleeve. He shook off her hand while Judge Shields pounded his gavel to quiet the spectators' voices rising in unison of their shock and surprise.

"Please, please," Zerelda whispered. She took to rapping the attorney's arm he couldn't ignore. She tried to keep her calm but knew her face gave away fear. "Please ask for a recess. I need to tell you something."

"Your Honor," her attorney yelled above the din after looking in her direction. "If it pleases the court, may I have a few minutes to speak with my client in private?"

"Ten minutes, and we are right back here." The judge turned to the witness and pointed the gavel in his direction. "Mr. Boronza, you remain seated here. Do not move."

Chapter Thirteen

October of 1907, Comedy of Confusion

"Zerelda," Mr. Cruickshank began as soon as they were seated in a small room across the hall from the courtroom. "Do you have something you wish to tell me?"

"Yes." She bowed her head, unable to look her attorney in the eyes, as she spoke. "Narcisco is up to his old tricks. He's telling a lie."

"How can you be sure?"

"I am positive," she responded. "He has brought a knife into the courtroom as evidence, but it can't be admitted."

"I'm confused."

"I used no knife," she answered. "But I had held something sharp."

"So does this mean you are remembering parts you've claimed so often gone from your memory?"

"I don't recollect much, but I do know what happened before so much blood filled the bedroom."

"Go on."

"I wanted to threaten him. He was making to leave me maybe for another woman, and I didn't want to be abandoned. I held something in my hand," Zerelda repeated in a near whisper. She looked down at her opened hands, puzzling they were empty.

"My God, woman," the attorney growled. "I based our entire defense on the fact you remembered nothing from the moment of your argument and him walking out of the house until Ella woke you. And now, you're telling me you threatened him? You knowingly lied to me?"

"I haven't lied as much as you think," she tried to rationalize. "I remember only what happened up to the moment I walked into the bedroom, and the stinking sot lay sprawled across the bed, not caring a twit of his filth. He was passed out from moonshine. We'd had yet another argument. I wanted to scare him."

"Scare him with what?"

"I had his straight razor in my hand," she replied. "No knife."

"A razor...you threatened your husband with a straight razor. Where is that weapon? Why do we not hold this in our possession, and why have you never told me any of this?"

"I thought..."

"You thought," he interrupted. "No one told you to think."

"I thought," she began again, "since my memory has failed me and Ella threw out his part that even the fact I'd walked into our bedroom might stay hidden."

"I'll ask you again. Where is the razor?"

"I don't know."

"You conveniently do not know where the straight razor is. But he has a knife here in the courtroom."

"My fingers found a razor after Ella woke me, and we looked at blood everywhere. The razor was stuck to the floor. I hid it without her noticing. At least I thought I did. A place I'd hoped to retrieve it from later." Her

112

answer had grown quieter with each word.

"I repeat. Where is the straight razor?"

"I hid it," she repeated.

Mr. Cruickshank dropped his head to his awaiting hands and remained so for a few minutes. Zerelda didn't dare move nor speak for fear of making him even more disappointed. Even with the day not even halfway passed, if her attorney asked for a recess until tomorrow based on this surprise new evidence, perhaps Mr. Cruickshank could come up with a solution. He must have come to a similar conclusion because he stood and waited for her to rise before escorting her toward the doorway. But he paused.

"You do not tell any of this to a soul. Do you understand?" Her attorney scowled as he spoke. "If, as you say, the razor cannot ever be found, there is no concrete evidence. I cannot tell the judge such information, or else your innocence will be at risk. The jury will scream *guilty* without hesitation. All I can do now is find someone to disavow the knife, such as the one Narcisco holds. I am going to ask for the court to reconvene tomorrow morning. You," he pointed a finger toward her face, "do not say a word."

****

"Mr. Boronza." The judge's voice left no room for interruption. He turned to the witness the next morning after Narcisco had struggled up the steps to the chair, making a grandiose show how feebled he'd become from his wound. "You are to be reminded you are still under oath."

"I have no further questions for my witness," Mr. Walton said after rising to his feet behind the table opposite Zerelda and her attorney.

"Nor do I," Mr. Cruickshank spoke up as soon as Judge Shields looked in his direction. The knife rested on display between the judge and attorneys' positions as evidence to the crime. Mr. Cruickshank left Narcisco with his mouth open in surprise and no chance to fabricate more stories. "I have no questions for this witness."

A spattering of comments reverberated from the spectator arena, causing the judge to bang the gavel. Again. He wielded it like a weapon.

Mr. Cruickshank didn't want to wait, though. "But your Honor, if it pleases the court," Attorney Cruickshank yelled over the noise. "I kindly ask the court to consider my calling one more witness."

Judge Shields raised his eyebrows. The judge either doubted no further questions of Narcisco as a good move or of the temerity to continue this charade by asking for a witness out of the natural order of cases conducted. The spectators held a collective breath for either the guilty to be exposed or for the judge to decide how to proceed.

"So be it," the judge said as he released a long-drawn-out sigh that had puffed out his cheeks. "One witness."

"If it pleases the court, I call Dr. Ashley B. Spencer to the stand."

Now the good doctor may have been considered by some as an excellent man of character, but others questioned his ability at such an advanced age. He neared eighty years old, had a white beard down to the middle of his chest, and wore a suit of clothes more apropos to Abraham Lincoln's attire he wore for his Gettysburg address. His shoulders bent forward as if in a permanent stage of picking up something, and he shuffled his feet, never quite lifting them from the floor. After a long five minutes of Narcisco stepping down and creeping back to the chair next to his attorney while Dr. Spencer shuffled his way to the witness stand, the crowd watched the doctor take the oath and scooch around on the hard chair to find some semblance of comfort.

Mr. Cruickshank picked up and held the knife Narcisco claimed to be the weapon Zerelda had used. He tapped the new evidence on his palm a couple of times. The snapping made a sound more like someone clucking for a horse to behave.

"Dr. Spencer, how are you today?"

"Right, good, Mr. Cruickshank. Glad to be above ground on this fine morning."

"Happy to hear. Do you know why we have called you to the stand today?"

"Yes." He nodded toward the knife in the attorney's hand and indicated he wanted to look at the item a bit closer. Mr. Cruickshank handed it over so the good doctor could bring the knife right up to within an inch of his nose. A ray of sunshine glinted off the blade as he twisted the knife back and forth. He worked his thumb across the cutting edge, twisted the wood grip over and back, and offered the handle end toward Mr. Cruickshank to take back.

"Now tell me, sir," the attorney began. He nonchalantly flipped the weapon back and forth from hand to hand. "Do you believe this knife can inflict the kind of injury we have been discussing during this court case?"

"No, I do not."

"Can you please explain?"

"Oh, I can explain until the cows come home, but I'd much rather show you." And with such an odd comment, he grabbed the handle of the knife back from the attorney, positioned the blade at the bottom of one earlobe, and pushed up in one swift movement as if he planned to cut off his ear in front of a crowded courtroom full of spectators. Nothing happened; no blood, and his ear still intact. The good doctor started to laugh, which soon became a loud cackling as he gazed out over the stunned audience. A couple sharp coughs interrupted his mirth. He cleared his throat with great and slow purpose. "This knife couldn't slice through the ripest watermelon, let alone a limb."

"Interesting," the attorney commented. A broad smile changed his entire demeanor while he kept nodding his head. The man looked to have found a pile of gold at his feet. His glee changed the air in the courtroom, and a few spectators tried without success to hold in snickers.

"He…" the doctor sputtered and pointed the knife at Narcisco, "continues to lie as he's done for all the years I've known him. A young lad loose on the streets, stealing pickles from the grocers' storefronts, and knocking over the water barrels for the horses. He's been a bad seed his whole life. Don't believe him even if he said the—"

"Thank you, Dr. Spencer. I think we get your point. This knife—the one they claim to be the weapon employed by my client—is worthless. Am I correct?"

The doctor nodded then uttered a definitive, "Yes."

"I contend we can rule this out as evidence." Mr. Cruickshank walked back to the table and stood next to

Zerelda. "Thank you for your expertise in this matter of great importance."

Dr. Spencer looked from Zerelda's attorney to Judge Shields and decided he must be done. He began the laborious task of leaving the witness chair and returning to the gallery.

"Your Honor, if it pleases the court, I have one more thing to say," Mr. Cruickshank continued before taking his seat.

From the judge's expression, not much pleased him anymore. But nothing stopped Zerelda's attorney from standing and walking to position himself between her and Judge Shields. He'd grabbed the lapels of his jacket and rocked to and fro on the heels and toes of his leather shoes as if about to recite the best joke known to man. He turned to face her and presented a huge smile as a gift before looping back toward the judge to say, "I rest my case."

"I beg your pardon?" Judge Shields' voice echoed strains of exasperation as he growled as loud as a bear. "You are choosing not to call any further witnesses? Not to fight for your client? To do nothing else?"

"Oh, I'll be doing something," the attorney replied. "Only not what you suggest. You will see in my closing statement why I feel my client is innocent and needs to be judged in accordance with the law as it is written." As before, he emphasized *innocence* instead of having the jurors hear anything relating to *guilt*.

The judge raised his gavel to quiet the crowd, belatedly realizing the need didn't exist. The room had fallen silent. This complete reversal of how most court cases proceed was so unheard of no one moved nor spoke. Zerelda felt as stunned as the rest and wondered if a prank had been played out in court with the jury serving as jesters. The silence felt as thick as Babcia's pea soup made to warm cold bones in the winter.

Chapter Fourteen

October of 1907, Curtain Call on a Trial

Mr. Benjamin Walton, attorney for Mr. Narcisco Boronza, sat down next to his client with a smile beaming on his face brighter than one being handed a blue ribbon for the fattest cow at the local fair. He never broke a sweat with all of his postulating. His closing statement had the jury sitting at attention no different than a pastor's flock being told the secret of getting into Heaven.

His so-called evidence placed the defendant at the scene of the crime, he reiterated the anger between husband and wife to the point his client appeared to be a saint while her the Devil in disguise, and he'd discredited Mr. Navarro's insinuation that the purchased knives were only for the husband's use. How ridiculous that a woman living in a house never cooked a meal! Or butchered meat for a meal. Or even had to wield a weapon against vermin. He conceded that yes, one needed a way to get rid of rats but wouldn't a trap have worked just as well? He contended she held a knife in hiding to use on her husband for when the mood struck her. He implied so many different ways she acted horribly to her husband that the jurors must have felt discombobulated on everything they heard.

In all his bluster, though, the plaintiff's attorney

had nothing more than *circumstantial evidence*—an intangible she could not be convicted on. But he did open a wound deep enough the jury may not have been able to think around it. Why hadn't she divorced Narcisco if she was so sure he was heading to another woman. Whether or not she had proof. The mere suggestion of her not taking a more civilized route would taste sour as the entire trial was rehashed by the jury.

The way he glanced over at Zerelda and her attorney, she imagined him counting out the years on his fingers and toes of how long the judge felt her incarceration might serve to send a message. But now her attorney's moment had arrived. To bring the desired results he'd so confidently impressed upon her.

Although she'd been shocked by his behavior in not calling more witnesses—not even allowing her to tell her side of the story—he'd assured her over and over again his closing statement would set her free.

Mr. Cruickshank meandered over to the jury box, where nine men and three women sat with all eyes on him, waiting for him to dispute Mr. Walton's claims. Two of the women glanced over toward Zerelda to give her quick nods and slight smiles. Three of the men scowled in her direction, as had been the case throughout the entire trial. Even when they appeared to be paying close attention to any discussion, the looks had continued to burn toward her.

"Ladies and gentlemen of the jury," he began. "On behalf of my client and of myself, thank you for your patience during this most unusual case. You have struggled through endless hours of listening to both my words and what Mr. Walton had to say. You've had to avoid speaking of this trial to all those questioning you outside of this room, and you have had to hear of details no one can ever prepare for. And yet, if you focused on the comments of Judge Shields, you will find my client innocent of all charges. A person cannot be convicted on *circumstantial evidence*. There is no weapon as we proved beyond a doubt, there are no eyewitnesses to this alleged crime, we have shown a man intent on intimidation, and there's no appendage to show as evidence. Who is to say for certain Mr. Narcisco Boronza lost his penis on the night in question? Maybe he needs to prove he actually had one prior to that time or prove he doesn't have one now! Think about it—there is no way to confirm the blood on my client wasn't hers after a vicious attack by him or someone else. Consider her running away could have come from sheer panic of not knowing what had happened."

He paused to let this long-winded soliloquy sink in. While his eyes roved over each juror, some returned eye contact while others squirmed in their seats. Some stared at something much more important on the floor or up at the ceiling.

"I repeat *circumstantial evidence*. Mr. Walton did not present to the court one iota of solid proof of my client as the perpetrator. You cannot convict but must let Mrs. Zerelda Boronza go free. As you adjourn to consider the testimony by these witnesses and the plaintiff's ill-advised presentation of a knife, please remember *if there is no real evidence, she does not have to pay penitence.*"

He repeated those thirteen words a couple more times as he made his way back to the table where Zerelda sat. He looked back at the jury, slowly sat down, and repeated, "If there is no real evidence, she does not have to pay penitence. I thank you for your patience and service."

Chapter Fifteen

November of 1907, Sitting in Judgment

Mayhem Trial to End Today, The Cedartown Review, November 5, 1907

Ten years ago, Narcisco Boronza introduced his new bride, one Zerelda Lena, to our village of Cedartown, and the residents of this sleepy little town embraced her with all the glory to be given of a home-grown son. She'd been welcomed and brought into the fold; her statuesque continence and beauty a pleasure to enjoy as she set up house and home for her new husband. Their ways were glorious in how they would comport their business and social events, how they'd travel to Lansing for affairs we mere mortals have no way of enjoying yet through what they'd impart on us, and how they brought a certain celebratory importance to our village.

And yet how sudden their lifestyle degraded and now, not even a decade later, how does she show her gratitude of those early days?

By committing Mayhem. Causing injurious harm too delicate of a subject to place in print but of the most horrendous of actions served upon her husband. And all this time, she claims innocence.

This reporter has attended every minute of the trial of Zerelda Lena Boronza and finds her guilty of the crime of Mayhem. She sits at the table of the accused; stiff, unbending, never an emotion crossing her features. She presents herself as a Queen and we her subjects. But it is not for me to claim her guilty. Or do you disagree? Should not every man find a woman guilty when committing any injustice against he who takes her in, furnishes her with clothing and food, gives her shelter? Should not a woman be grateful and serve her husband with love and honor, not disrespect?

The jury has been sequestered overnight and has summoned Judge T.W. Shields twice for additional information. Now fourteen hours later, the jury is prepared to give their decision. Are we, as citizens of this village of Cedartown, ready to accept?

****

Mr. Cruickshank folded the newspaper in half before Zerelda brought her gaze down to the tabletop.

"Mrs. Zerelda Lena Boronza. Please rise and hear the judgment placed upon you by a jury of your peers." Judge Shields didn't even bother to look up from papers in front of him.

She didn't want to stand. Zerelda wanted to run from the courtroom, screaming at the top of her lungs, and hide in the small cell she'd spent the last few weeks in. She wanted to magically go back to her life before meeting Narcisco. Back when her dreams of becoming a dazzling Gibson Girl filled her thoughts. Back to her big dreams.

But this had to end. *Dearie, all will work out. The best you can do is not think, not wonder, not imagine, nor even obsess. Just breathe and have faith all will work out for the best.* Her Babcia's voice echoed inside Zerelda's head. *Breathe. Fill your lungs.*

The foreman, an elderly man with a handlebar mustache sweeping wide and curling over each cheek, cleared his throat and stood. He had the expression creasing his face of a man heading for a guillotine. Not of having to speak a few words proscribed by the jury of twelve. Moments earlier, he'd shown the slip of paper to Judge Shields as custom dictated. The judge reviewed it and then handed it back to the foreman, who took the paper and returned to stand by his chair. A man standing at attention, waiting for the shot to be taken by a firing squad.

Zerelda and her attorney leaned forward in unison. Mr. Cruickshank once again covered her hand with his and gave a slight squeeze. Her lungs constricted, and her heart palpitated.

"Guilty," the foreman blurted out. "Guilty of Mayhem in the first degree of causing injurious harm to another human being."

Zerelda stiffened. The foreman sat down as a volley of hoots and howls erupted from spectators, but when Zerelda turned to look, her gaze landed on Corey and Ella. They'd both, as if in tandem, bowed their faces into their hands and rocked to and fro. Some perverted type of justice had been meted out but clearly not what her own attorney had assured her of. How many times had he told her *circumstantial evidence* would be the key to winning this case—nothing solid. No convictable substance. But he'd been proven otherwise.

The jury had found the witnesses credible enough to find her guilty of a crime she had no memory of. Hiding guilt was impossible to pretend as none resided within her. The only moments existing were the argument of a fateful evening, her walking into the bedroom to look upon a drunken husband while she held a straight razor in one hand and surprised to wake at Ella's soft but insistent words. And of shoving the razor covered in dried blood under a nightstand. Maybe all the gore proved too much for the jury to bear, and someone had to pay the price.

"Mrs. Narcisco—nee Zerelda—Boronza," Judge Shields sliced his voice through the crowds. They quieted without a bang of the gavel. So many wanted to hear every single word spoken. "You have been found guilty of the crime of Mayhem by a jury of your peers. Do you have anything to say before I determine sentencing?"

Zerelda looked over to her attorney, who now when she needed his direction the most, presented a sterling imitation of a statue. He'd pulled his hand from hers as soon as the word *guilty* left the foreman's mouth. He stared straight ahead toward the judge's bench with his palms splayed on the table in front of him. The only sign he wasn't stiff as concrete being the sound of his shoes tapping in agitation.

"Do I have anything to say?" she whispered to the man she'd placed all her confidence in. Even choosing to believe him that taking the stand in her own defense might have worked against them. Mr. Cruickshank's concern being how the opposing attorney twisted words as destructive as a hell-bent tornado. He'd have taken her answers of no memories from the night-in-question as a way of her gaining the jury's sympathies, making Narcisco the innocent and her as vengeful. The jury members were left uninformed of her absolute fears of abandonment, reprisal, and abuse.

Being able to declare her innocence at the beginning of the trial but at no other time had proved disastrous. After such a long and drawn-out week of testimony, no wonder the jury saw her guilty. Her claim had fallen on deaf ears. The jury proved how soon details can be forgotten. "Mr. Cruickshank, tell me what to do. What was *if there is no real evidence, she does not have to pay penitence* all about if they say I'm guilty? Please, please…"

He cleared his throat and came back to the living, bowing his head in defeat. From the corner of his mouth, he whispered back, "Accept your sentence."

"Please no…"

Chapter Sixteen

February of 1908, Months of Cruel Awakenings

A new prisoner arrived from the small village of Cedartown.

Never been there myself but heard tell it's a sleepy little burgh. Not much going on, but then every town has its secrets. And now this here woman shows up with a most unusual story. She got herself a sentence of five years for, dare I write it down, whacking off her husband's plum-tree shaker. Guess we know what he won't be doing from now on. She wasn't very talkative when I told her what we expected. Said she understood the rules and had grown tired of having everyone repeat them. I, as quickly, reminded her she'd like the rules a whole lot less if she don't follow them. Probably haven't heard the last of this one and will bear keeping an eye out. Three months have gone by, and all's quiet at this point.

~Warden Pervis, February 5, 1908

****

If there is no real evidence, she does not have to pay penitence.

Not true. Now she sat alone, forced to atone with seconds, minutes, hours, and months behind steel rods rattling as incessant as the chiming of a clock each time a cell door down the line was pulled open or clanged closed. Ten cells on this floor with two other floors she'd never been allowed to walk. She counted from one to ten with the passing of each cell, multiplying the number by three. Upward of thirty females in the women's prison. The men's hoosegow had inmates into the hundreds.

Three marches each day—once for a meal of grayish mush the warden loved to begin the day with, a second time for a lunch of lukewarm soup made from ingredients most oftentimes unidentifiable and paired with a slice of bread, and a third repast for a late supper to hold each woman until the next morning. Day after day, the routine repeated without variation.

The Women's State Prison of Jackson was located a stone's throw from the men's side, which she'd heard crammed more in with smaller cells. Maybe even uglier. The structure still stood years later, even if the whole place looked slapped together as temporary quarters. Hard to imagine a stark setting worse than this one with cockroaches freely moving from cell to cell. In a world of the brilliant greens of grass and leaves, sunshine yellow, and bright red cabooses, plus the extraordinary mauves and purples of her bonnets, this place dulled the senses. Slate gray cement floors, brackish-gray steel bars, and murky gray clothing. Even the foul-smelling food slopped onto colorless trays seemed tinged with gray.

What she'd learned of the machinations within these walls came from rumors and gossip. Words were passed down from women taking care of laundry and meals for the men. Her time had not come of these chores being pressed upon her. Word circulated that being tasked to wash and cook was considered a privilege for good behavior.

She had other schemes for passing the time, something useful so as not to go as crazy as prisoner number 483. Clara by name. How that woman rambled on night after bloody night about taking care of the garden, pulling weeds large enough to bury a mountain, digging trees enough to dam up a river, and animals feasting on carrion. If prisoner numbers were any indication, Zerelda being 22701, Clara had been behind these bars long enough for twenty seasons of gardens to go unattended.

With nights blurring one into another, her idle hands itched to be creative. She'd dream of beautiful bonnets coming to life under her needle and thread expertise. Many nights the thought of nothing to live for sent her spiraling down a forlorn path with no end in sight. A thought began to percolate. A seed of an idea growing every morning yet split Zerelda in two directions. What about making bonnets for the women inmates? But what about staying invisible? Not bringing attention to herself.

They'd been photographed upon entrance to the prison but oh, how horrible each woman must have looked. Was she brave enough to make a difference? A beautiful bonnet, a little care and treatment, and then a new picture for the annals of the prison could make her time between these walls mean something. But where to start? Where even to get more fabric? She'd eventually found a source to experiment with.

Next, an audience with the warden, Mr. H. Pervis, seemed the most logical. Yet the specter of failure hung at the edges of her idea like a cliff she could slip over. Most evenings for the past three months, Zerelda had asked the night watchman to please pass along a message of wanting an audience with the warden. She failed to disclose what she wanted to discuss, and maybe her reticence proved to be the stumbling block.

Tonight, she'd tease him with a seldom-offered smile and a few select words to perhaps pique his interest. Something about newspapers, goodwill, and photographs. In the meantime, she had a couple hours by her calculations based on shadows inching across the walls to continue working on a cloth braid.

"Zerrie," she heard from the woman across the narrow hall. Wondrous, she called herself, inmate 22694. The woman couldn't have been much more than sixteen years old—too young to be lost in this place. Wondrous blinked her eyes so often as if to clear away dust it made Zerelda tired watching her, and she felt convinced the young gal told lies easier than admitting the truth. Her name possibly being the best example! Whoever had heard of such a name? But at least they'd had a few interesting conversations. "You in there? Been pretty quiet today."

"I'm here. Ready for your questions."

Since their incarceration, the two of them ending up together on the train from Howell to Jackson, they'd become as close as friends found each other in this hellhole. Zerelda and Wondrous had clasped hands with each other after enduring the degradation of having to strip down to their shifts in order for guards to rub their grimy hands up and down their bodies. Weapons or maybe sweets being the hoped-for prize. They'd even flinched in unison. The long walk past cells full of women moaning or crying, begging for forgiveness or singing, or turning away their faces as one sat over the metal honey pot or spit up bile from the previous meal became subject matter for their first whispered conversation. Their talks always started moments after the doors to each cell had been latched, and the guard walked away. They'd wait for him to be out of earshot and particularly when he started whistling. She'd soon realized this habit during nightly rounds gave an impression of not having a care in the world.

"Heard you got more cloth," Wondrous whispered. "Are you ever going to tell me what you're workin' on?"

"Soon," Zerelda answered as her fingers flew over and under the three strands of linen cloth. Each finished braid ranged from six to twelve inches and secured at each end with knots. Before creating a braid, she'd take great care to unravel strands out of the fraying fabric to make each length of cloth feathery looking. Sometimes she wound the braid so tight the fabric compressed to a flat rope. Oftentimes the material worked better if held together loosely to create a puffy look. More along the lines of a boa used by dancers on stage as they covered areas of their voluptuous shapes. If only bonnet bases were available. Oh, the glorious hats to be created—ethereal, plumose and light, and as elegant and airy as old fabric could appear.

The women working in the laundry area smuggled old rags and used tattered towels, sometimes even a rare feed bag not grabbed up earlier, to her under cover of their own clean towels. She'd work on these braids a few minutes at a time, always aware the guards gamed at sneaking down the hallway unheard and unnoticed. They seemed to delight in catching women in the act of doing something against the rules. If caught, punishment behind these bars came swift and harsh and then rarely spoken about for fear of making the cruelty real for everyone.

But Zerelda pressed on. Once a braid met her satisfaction, she'd squeeze the rope between the mattress and frame. So far, those already hidden away hadn't changed the look of the mattress from a distance but, with each passing day, concern pressed in on her of being found out. That was the worrisome part—of being discovered and punished before having a chance to talk with the warden.

"How about a story?" Wondrous inquired. Their stories were spoken in muted tones most nights to help the long hours pass.

"Maybe I need to tell you about my travels with Narcisco to Lansing." Zerelda didn't hear any complaint from the next cell, so she continued. "We had money, and oh how he boasted. Ever heard of the Hotel Downey?"

"Have," Wondrous whispered. "Never been there."

"Went to a party there," Zerelda said, then paused with her tale to tuck away another braid. She picked up more cloth. "We walked in the front door as special as royalty like a king and queen. Oh, Narcisco put on fussy airs searching out what he desired most—attention and gifts. Guess we all know he won me with his ways. Anyhow, we were there for a party to celebrate the new governor held in the Victory Room on the second floor. Everywhere we saw buntings of red, white, and blue hanging from banisters, walls, and even the mirror behind the massive bar. Late into the evening, after more drinks than I could remember and so much food, we went to our rooms on the sixth floor.

The sights were amazing being so high up. "

"Bet you looked so pretty that night."

Zerelda had. She'd watch as heads turned their way whenever she and Narcisco entered a crowded room. Didn't matter if it was in a restaurant or entering a bar, or waltzing into a ballroom. Such gratification fed her dreams of truly being a famous actress. The only time focus seemed to be elsewhere would be at the moment waiters paraded into the restaurant holding trays high on their shoulders filled with petite orange omelets, oysters on the half shell, smoked oysters wrapped in bacon, and generous slices of Lady Baltimore cake. What a sight to behold.

But the mood of the room cooled as fast as an unexpected north wind. Whispers began to circulate. Strange looks came their way, and most stopped making eye contact while others turned their backs on them without comment. Left them puzzled at first. Unkind words seeped through the room like a devious mist of their dwindling funds, rumors of how they never paid for anything nor donated to campaigns, and always expected favors, with nothing in return from them.

At the end of one such otherwise exquisite evening in another restaurant, the waiter had slipped the handwritten bill under Narcisco's elbow—$9.15 for the seven-course meal they'd just finished. Her husband gazed down at the slip of paper and up toward the waiter's retreating back. He'd shook his head, and she sensed trouble from that moment on.

They never carried coins except for the few to flip at a porter or doorman, and they had no way of paying for the dinner. Within minutes and with a detached insistence, they were escorted out the front door and asked to never return.

"Zerrie, you still there?"

"Oh yes, sorry," she replied. Her hands had stilled at the memory of such a short time ago when their sumptuous life had been as easy as plucking a ripe apple in an orchard of trees as far as the eye could see. A party without end. Until Narcisco had foolishly drained their reserves and kept it a secret from her. "I did look beautiful until I no longer had use for those dresses."

"What happened?"

"I wish I knew. Narcisco changed."

The evening train rumbled to a stop alongside the prison delivering supplies or more prisoners. The cars would be emptied out and then filled back up with everything manufactured behind the stone walls, from pottery to furniture, carded buttons to rugs, to bricks to clothing. The timetable was better than clockwork as each day ended, a low hum resounding through the thick walls, all from the clattering of the cast-iron wheels riding the rails. Single light bulbs strung along the ceilings would shake and sway. This night the lights flickered before plunging them into blackness. Groans and a couple wails echoed from various cells as silence soon cloaked the women under a dark blanket. Guessing started as inmates whispered seconds and minutes of how long the darkness would shroud them. Sometimes the wait lasted until dawn.

Zerelda tucked the unfinished braid under the mattress below her. She stretched out, figuring to wait out the darkness while crushing the braids with her slight frame. She worried as the bulk increased and the bed became more comfortable. Someone might notice and become suspicious.

Time to pursue with greater persistence an audience with the warden.

Chapter Seventeen

March of 1908, Cracking While Killing Time

One of the longest-serving inmates seems to be mentally cracking. As I walked by this evening, she whispered through the bars about hands seen by her alone coming into the cell to burn and torment.

Always operated under the theory this place was a prison. But the longer I move through these darkened walkways and stand at doorways of the mess hall and listen to crack-pots and cranks as they yell their demands, the more I'm convinced we run an insane asylum as over half of these prisoners sink toward lunacy. They sit or sleep in their cells all day instead of having to do any work. They insistently hawk, rattle, and holler all night long even though the rule of silence can bring punishment.

This woman grew louder, and her noise echoed throughout the chamber as the night progressed. I fear there may be no choice but to send her to the Ionia Insane Asylum.

~Warden Pervis, March 17, 1908

****

Gnarled fingers gripped the bars catching Zerelda's gaze as she passed by the cell down the corridor from hers. The woman's eyes glared daggers at anyone passing by.

"Know what you're doing." The inmate's voice hissed like a snake louder than the skittering rush of a couple rats along the cell wall. "Won't help 'cause of what you did."

Zerelda shuffled her thin boots to move quicker and stubbed her big toe into a prisoner's heel ahead of her. She could feel pain shoot up her leg as her toe bent upward at a harsh angle.

"Sorry," she mumbled before being able to stop herself. Her attorney—poor befuddled Mr. Cruickshank—had warned her while still reeling from the guilty verdict of three rules to remember while behind bars. Three ways to come out of this alive. This advice coming during his one and only visit to the prison a month after her incarceration.

Rule one: keep your eyes trained downward unless asked a question by a guard or warden. If that happens, look the guard in the eye and be quick with your answer.

Rule two: whisper when speaking to any other prisoner so as not to be heard by the guards. Speaking when out from behind of the bars of their cells was verboten. Silence meant invisibility.

Rule three: keep a nail secured in her dress hem or cuff to defend herself if attacked but never let it be discovered.

He'd murmured this third rule while never taking his gaze off her face. Then, while remaining as still as possible, he'd slipped a four-inch blunt steel spike under his palm across the table to her awaiting hand. The guard had not even detected wrongdoing with how surreptitiously they'd brought fingertips together and made the transfer.

The cold metal shaft had stung her palm as memories of a straight razor glinted off through her thoughts. Her surprise at his temerity caused a shiver to run the length of her spine.

And now tingling danced along her spine as the two women made eye contact. Zerelda looked downward as quick as possible, remembering her attorney's admonitions but not before the old woman's deep green eyes reminded Zerelda danger lurked in dark corners of these dingy cells.

"'Member my number," the old woman whispered and pointed a twisted finger to her chest where a worn patch showed 692, "'cause your back ain't safe 'round here." She let wasted hands slip down to hang at her sides as the weight of death pulled her closer to the ground. "Your man has friends in this place."

Zerelda figured her for a *spook*—a talker in prison with nothing to back up any threats—but she never could be certain her husband didn't have connections. Better to avoid this one.

The nail nestled between two seams at the hem of Zerelda's loose dress. It brushed along her ankle, getting caught on stocking fabric enough for the end to scrape at her skin. She rustled the skirt to loosen any contact hoping no one noticed her wince. The possibility of using the rusty shaft felt real and even imminent. Since her attorney had given her this weapon, she'd fingered it a couple of times more as a talisman than a means of protection.

"Don't want no problems," Zerelda whispered. The rule of silence proved hard to follow, with everyone needing to tell their story, find companionship in conversation, or scream. Or harass and intimidate with words. She understood, but that didn't make any of this any easier.

The line began moving again toward the north hall, where a meal awaited them. Wondrous followed right on her heels, so no doubt she'd heard the exchange. There'd be questions later.

As they shuffled farther down the walkway, stale air hung rancid from unemptied pots while low spots in the floor held brown, thick puddles looking like overflow from those same vessels. Zerelda held in a gag rising up from her empty stomach, desperate to keep the guards' prying eyes from bringing unwanted attention. They stepped into the massive hall and filed past the counter to grab a plate containing a small chunk of cheese, something grayish-brown resembling beef, and a piece of bread. Her stomach responded with a growl of hunger, even if the entire meal looked to have been drying out most of the afternoon.

The room seemed eerily quiet for the large number of women sitting at long tables hunched over their plates of food. Three of the walls had barred windows at the first level and then two levels upward of cells with walkways surrounding the hall at the outer edges. These cells housed men as if they were animals in a zoo. Quite a few of them stood with their hands clasping the bars watching the females. The air felt thick from unspoken words, but punishment would come swift for any hoots or hollers or even whispers.

"What are you going to do?" Wondrous sat down, kept her head bowed toward the plate, and asked her question before giving attention to her food.

Zerelda also kept her gaze trained on the unappetizing plate of food, but between a couple bites of the meat, she mumbled, "Ignore the old bat."

"But you heard her. She's out for you."

Zerelda gently nudged Wondrous' hand closer to the spoon next to the plate, so the young gal caught hold of the utensil instead of patting fingers across the table. Her eyesight was bad enough but always worse when something rattled her. This place had a way of unsettling even the most stout-hearted, let alone drowning someone as fragile as Wondrous.

"Can't do anything that'll draw attention to me," Zerelda replied. She peered down the long table to see if prisoner number 692 sat anywhere close.

As if on cue, the old woman looked up from her own food and made eye contact once again with Zerelda. *Rule number one: keep your eyes downward.* She bowed her head as quick as possible, hoping not to draw attention to herself, and concentrated on working her teeth through some gristle.

"Let's talk later."

****

"You scared?"

"Aw, Wondrous," Zerelda replied. She hoped her voice sounded braver on the outside than it did inside her brain. The old woman—prisoner number 692—had in fact made her fear Narcisco's reach extended from Cedartown across all the miles southwest of Lansing to Jackson. If his attorney hadn't placed a hand on Narcisco's arm, she knew for certain he'd have whooped and laughed in her direction at the moment of conviction. The look of glee radiating from his face mimicked a kid getting all the candy in the world. Fortunately, with his show of delight, payback had come quick when he jerked a bit too suddenly, resulting in a pained look to crumple his face into ugliness. With that first look of triumph, remorse left her like birds taking flight. He'd gotten what he deserved. "You worry too much. We're safe behind these bars."

Comments had filtered to her ears from spectators whispering she deserved some kind of comeuppance. Still, others questioned if she received enough punishment.

Mayhem.

Judge Shields had enunciated each word of the charge as if she didn't understand the English language. Mayhem—the crime of disabling, disfiguring, rendering useless a member of another person's limbs, and the injury must be permanent, not a temporary loss. What Narcisco lost could not be replaced. But it now seemed between Narcisco and the whole trial debacle, she'd also suffered a permanent loss. Her freedom.

"Boronza...Zerelda...Prisoner Number 22701." The booming voice echoed down the walkway past all of the metal cages to the back wall and bounced off the end wall into Zerelda's cell. "Boronza...you have a visitor. Wave your hand through the bars so I can find you."

Arms and even some legs were thrust through the bars of nearly every cell faster than a rabbit can escape a hawk. Hoots and hollers rose to a crescendo as the wave of sound reverberated off the walls and floor. The guard waited until the women grew bored and drew in their arms and legs to retire back to their minutes, hours, and days. Zerelda cautiously put her left arm between the bars and gave a wave toward Mr. Pervis. Surprise at seeing the warden instead of the usual nightwatchman left her rattled. Her hands shook as she smoothed down her loose-fitting dress, patted at her frazzled hair, and furtively touched the nail at the hem of the smock to make sure it wasn't loose. She knew the smart thing to do meant tucking it inside the mattress, but the warden's heels clicked on the concrete floor as he strode down the walkway. He came to a quick halt in front of the cell.

"Zerelda Boronza?"

"Yes."

"Let me see your patch so I can read the number."

Zerelda threw back her shoulders, so the numbers *22701* showed inches above her left breast.

"You have a visitor. This is highly unusual to allow anyone here in the evening, but this is at the pleasure of the court." Warden Pervis' gaze had lingered on the patch and number, making it clear following these orders left a bad taste in his mouth. He rattled the ring usually hooked to his belt until he found the one etched with her cell number and inserted the key into the lock. He pulled open the door. "Come along now."

He stepped back and motioned for Zerelda to move into the walkway. As instructed during her and Wondrous' arrival, always walk ahead of the warden instead of being escorted. This positioned the guard or warden in the best place to subdue a prisoner if any thoughts of escape entered their mind. Ha...as if she could run away. After the first month of malnutrition and little chance to move around except for an hour each day wandering around a small courtyard, her gait had slowed to a shuffle giving her no doubts to arguing or inciting a problem. Her thoughts instead jangled as they passed each of the numerous cells as to whether or not the timing proved right to broach the project weighing on her mind.

"You in trouble now, dearie." The cackling voice came from the old woman. Prisoner number 692. "Watch your step."

Zerelda held her head high, snubbing the threat. A lifetime had passed since Mr. Cruickshank's single visit a few days after her arrival here. No one else, not even Corey Strayer, had shown up, and Zerelda had stopped hoping. Not many of the women had visitors; those left behind no doubt, having moved on with their lives. Or at least trying to survive without the convicted in their lives. Yet someone waited in a room for her—either her attorney, maybe Corey, perhaps Ella, but that seemed improbable. Someone, though, was interested in her well-being or at least curious of these living conditions. She relished the thought of seeing anyone at this point.

"Sir?" Zerelda couldn't let the moment pass as she led the warden. "I'd like to ask something of you."

"This isn't a social walk," he replied.

"I understand, but I've been wanting to speak with you for weeks. Has the guard not mentioned my request?"

"He has."

"So can I ask?"

"Might as well."

"I make hats, you know, such as bonnets for women."

"Not a question I might point out."

"My question," she began after taking a deep breath so the words could spill out uninterrupted. "Can I make bonnets for the ladies here in prison, and can we take photographs of them? Give them something to be proud of."

Nothing; no sound from the man walking behind her. As much as temptation raged within to turn her head to see if he'd heard, a suspected act of aggression might ruin her chances.

"My question to you," he spoke, after sending a stream of spittle off to the side, "where do we come up with hats?"

Zerelda smiled. At least he hadn't dismissed the idea out of hand. She dared not mention all of the braids residing under her mattress for fear of retribution. They had reached the end of the long walkway and were about to turn into the stairwell. What if she turned around and let her thoughts tumble out before they reached the next floor? Would he listen or punish? Before another moment passed, a hand clamped her left shoulder, shoving her forward. She stubbed her sore toe on a crack and stumbled forward a couple steps.

"Keep moving with eyes forward."

Once out of the stairwell, Warden Pervis stepped up alongside her and pointed toward the door to the room where she'd met her attorney. The door had wooden latticework where glass may have once been but now only open spaces. He swung the door outward, and she stepped through the archway, coming face to face with a stranger. Well, maybe not a complete stranger. He seemed familiar, but she couldn't place him.

The man stood as she entered the room. He motioned for her to sit down in the chair across the table from where he'd been. The warden closed the door but remained standing in the hallway within hearing distance. Zerelda sat down and placed her hands in her lap, waiting for him to speak.

Chapter Eighteen:

March of 1908, Destiny Presents a Gift

Last night one of the women spoke directly at me. Inmate 692 has been here too long.

I'm not a man disposed to warnings and the unknown, but she seemed otherworldly. Her speech garbled through tight lips, and her eyes seemed lit from behind.

"Don't stare at me, Pervis. Makes me feel you're undressing me with your eyes. I'm not a woman prone to such excesses, you know, and you make me feel ashamed." I walked on, but she continued to mumble, "I'm as good as the queen of England, but you've decided I'm a quisby—you know what I'm saying! You callin' me a lazy woman with your eyes. Ain't right, you know."

There's been talk of towels going missing, and maybe these convicts are trying to take me off the sniff. I fear our nightwatchman will need to be on guard with more enthusiasm. Or we need to work our female inmates—always figure a tired prisoner is a good prisoner.

~Warden Pervis, March 21, 1908
****

"As beautiful as I remember; *statuesque*."

Zerelda startled at his first words and raised up a

hand to snarled hair before she could stop. Her thoughts were flustering all in a jumble. He remembered her. What a strange comment. She knew nothing of him. She looked back toward the door of the small room spotting the warden's back, figuring he remained to listen for any suspicious conversation. A scream would reach his ears if this visit was anything but friendly.

"I beg your pardon? May I ask who you are and what you want?" To be perfectly honest, she'd been hoping for someone she knew. A recognizable face before her, not a stranger wanting to gawk. Dealing with prisoners taunting her made for dreadful moments, but now she suspected Narcisco of sending strangers to intimidate her.

"You don't remember me," he stated without any guile or conceit.

Zerelda shook her head and remained still waiting for more information. She wasn't about to give away anything. The room they were in felt no larger than her cell. The room felt crowded with a table, two chairs, and two adults. Left no space to move around or for one to look away. Instead, she stared across the table at him and willed this man to get to the point.

"I attended your trial. You looked me straight in the eyes, or at least I believed that to be the case."

"There were too many spectators who came to watch. To revel in my suffering." She pushed back the chair, preparing to stand.

He put out a hand to beg her to remain. She wavered but moved one foot toward the door. Having any conversation regarding the disastrous trial failed to win her confidence in speaking to anyone, including this interloper.

"Did my husband send you to witness his revenge in action? State your business now, or I summon the warden."

"Please," the man begged. "I'm such a sot. Let me start over. I am *not* here on behalf of your husband, and I'm *not* one of the curious." He paused and allowed the edges of a smile to appear on his lips. "Well, maybe a bit intrigued."

Zerelda squirmed about not so much wanting to draw the warden's attention but more not to allow this man to believe he'd won her curiosity. After considering her choices of going back to the dark, dank cell or talking with this visitor, the realization hit her she had filled her lungs with fresher air and even sat up a little straighter. A few minutes away from the three grimy walls and a row of unyielding bars lifted a burden she now carried since arriving.

This man, pleasant enough to look at, sat still with his brown hair smoothed back from deep-set blue eyes, an aquiline nose, and lips curling into a slight smile across his clean-shaven face while she looked him over. There might have even been a couple nicks from the razor if one looked close enough. The brown fedora he'd poised on the table matched flawlessly to the dark suit jacket draped on his well-defined chest.

"You claim you attended my trial. Why?"

He released a short laugh as if he had won this go-round and reached down to lift up a satchel from the floor. A cockroach hung on tight to the top of the briefcase. He flicked the pest with his forefinger and thumb, sending the brown bullet across the room. It hit the wall and fell to the floor. They both watched as the cockroach seemed unfazed and scurried along the floor toward the gap under the door.

"Problem much with roaches?"

Zerelda scrunched her nose at his question and his ignorance of any problems existing in this horrible place. Some of the male prisoners had taken to drawing pictures of the filthy cockroaches for the prison newspaper—the *Spectator*—of men smoking them with as much relish as a real cigar. Cigars and cigarettes replaced with vermin. She had tried to kill a few in the cell after listening for their scurrying along the floor once the lights were turned off. She'd wait with one foot at the ready to squash whatever noise came by while she lay stretched out on the mattress. How far she'd come not to be appalled by any of this.

"I doubt you are here to solve the problem of cockroaches in prison," Zerelda answered.

He glanced back down at the briefcase as if he'd forgotten why they were in this room together. He released the latch, pushing the flap open, and drew out a piece of what looked to be a sketch on canvas. After holding the piece in front of his face and gazing at it with admiration, he turned the item around toward Zerelda. A mirror image of herself floated before her eyes. Only not as worn down as she now imagined her appearance presented itself. She raised trembling fingers toward the charcoal or pencil drawing, yet not touching the paper for fear her image could fade away. She sat mesmerized and unable to move.

"Did you draw this?" She spoke without lifting her gaze upward.

He didn't respond, so she looked up. He was nodding while allowing a broader smile to crinkle his cheeks.

"You drew this of me during the trial? How? When?"

"You honestly do not recognize me?"

This time she remained silent and just shook her head back and forth.

"Imagine me with a long beard and a moustache."

Second by second, the blue of his eyes surrounded by too much hair worked their way through her thoughts. "You were one of the first three jurors to be placed?"

"Yes."

"So, you were on the jury." In her mind's-eye, the three men all looked identical, giving her no clue which one he was.

"Yes."

"And found me guilty." She drew her hand back and left it poised in the air as if her muscles had taken on a life of their own. As she tensed, a memory flashed through her head stronger than lightning of the last time her muscles shook. It was that day of her sentencing. The afternoon her life changed, although the bits and pieces of why were as scattered as chicken feed in the dirt. She brought her hand down to the tabletop so hard a stinging slap resounded through the small room. Her head pounded with realization a person could sit across from her, oblivious in his own innocence against a guilty judgment.

Silence bounced between them as a look of puzzlement creased his face at her quick response.

"Tell me something," Zerelda continued, "tell me why you are here."

"I..."

"Why conversing with you is important for me.

Did you fool yourself into believing bringing me a drawing of a time best forgotten will make me feel better? And like you?"

She stood so fast the chair teetered on its back legs. No more cajoling to change her mind. She backed up toward the door. "How can you be so brash?"

He held up both hands guilty as a criminal caught in the act and surrendering for mercy.

"You've got-t-t everything all-l-l wrong," he stuttered. "Please sit back down."

"*I* have misunderstood? *I* have it all wrong? A jury of my supposed peers found me guilty with absolutely no evidence to back their decision. You included."

"I do not believe you committed Mayhem on your husband." The man's voice was thick with remorse.

"Tell me why I'm sitting in this prison—have been for months—while my husband plays the victim. Can you?"

"I believed right along you were involved in whatever happened yet still innocent. Self-defense— your attorney should have pressed for a lesser charge."

"I repeat…why am I here?"

"Please, let's begin again. Can I tell you my name? Please give me a chance to tell you what happened."

The warmth of the floor seeping through her thin boots gave her pause on storming out with all her indignation intact. Maybe prolonging moments of being anywhere else but traveling the catwalk and standing in her cell would serve her better. Oh, if only her attorney sat before her or the welcoming faces of Corey and Ella. Indecision worked against her.

She had to admit to being egocentric and maybe no more narcissistic than her husband as she thought of her own happiness. Had she put herself in this position by her own actions of not thinking of others? Too much time to think between these walls. If she'd walked away from Narcisco instead of confronting him, what would her life be now? Why hadn't she jumped on the closest bicycle a day earlier and traveled for parts unknown? She should have been the one to desert him. She may not have been any better off, but she'd not be under lock and key.

What gave her the right to fault this one man for her bad choices?

With nothing of urgency looming on the horizon, the prospect of enjoying the warmth of this room overruled all other thought. Hear him out. She'd keep trust at bay, knowing his actions earlier helped to put her in this decrepit old building. She found her head bobbing up and down before her brain had informed her of the decision to hear him out.

"Louis," he offered up before she changed her mind. "Louis, but my friends call me Louie. Last name of Lewski." He smiled again and shrugged. "I think by the time my parents had me after naming eleven, they'd stopped worrying about names so much."

"Well, Mr. Louis Lewski. Tell me why listening to anything you say is in my best interest." Zerelda sat back down before the warden came in. She let some of the stiffness in her back relax against the chair and waited for him to continue.

Louie tapped nervous fingers on the drawing spread between them. "Can I explain how disheartening I felt chosen to be on a jury where all of the members—the three women included—had already made up their minds long before the trial even began?"

"But you had doubts?" Now she wondered if he was the one who wouldn't look at Narcisco's attorney during his closing statement.

"I did, and I expressed them during the recesses from the courtroom."

"Mr. Lewski, if you'd be so kind, tell me how you justified finding me guilty."

"Two reasons," he answered. "First off, the trial needed to end. These men and those women had to be allowed to resume their lives. Changing their minds would have been like telling a bull it had no business being with a cow in heat."

He started to open his mouth to say more but then at least had the decency to blush at his inappropriate comment.

"Resume their lives...interesting way to view everyone else but me."

"Our lives are not our own. What we do every day makes a difference in someone else's," he spoke. "Make money, prepare meals, hold children at the end of the day. These people had to get back to taking care of those in their lives."

"Let me get this straight. You decided my life served as less important than theirs. I couldn't possibly have someone to take care of? You know nothing of me, yet you presume to know everything about those you sat with."

Louie bowed his head in acknowledgement.

"You allowed your peers to judge me on implications and false information."

"Yes. For those few moments of my indiscretion, I am forever sorry."

"Well, I cannot accept your apology."

"May I tell you the second reason?"

Instead of nodding, she continued to stare in his direction.

"We called Judge Shields into the room, and I requested to know what kind of sentence you'd receive if convicted of Mayhem."

"And?"

"All of us were in the room, and together we heard the same sentence. The law required at most three years with possible parole after one year and at the least the time you sat in the local lock-up. I admit now I played the odds of the judge letting you off with a light sentence. With time to reflect, I see the error of my ways believing the judge would be gracious due to no solid evidence and of how so few women…"

"You *played the odds* with my life. You watched as a courtroom full of men yelled and hooted of me deserving the death sentence. You sat there day after day while that attorney tore my life to shreds and built up my husband's character to make him look like a saint. You *played the odds* of my being a woman protecting me? Do you believe all this twaddle you spew at me? A woman having a right for a fair trial when this is a man's world?"

"Please, Zerelda, I mean Mrs. Boronza, you misunderstand."

"Oh, believe me when I say I fully understand," she said. She was on her feet faster than he could apologize again. "You have shown me how you were cowed into agreeing to a guilty verdict, so now I am done having you sit here trying to convince me anything you say is worth hearing. Guard! Warden Pervis, please may I go back to my cell?"

"But...I...I," Louis stammered. He also rose to his full height, inches taller than her as his eyes pleaded for her to grasp his sincerity. The sketch rustled upon their quick rising and slid to the floor as limp as a bird with a broken wing. He blurted out, "I came to ask your permission to do something on your behalf."

She denied him a chance to continue as she swept out of the room with as much dignity as the old gray rag of a dress allowed, muttering under her breath, "I'll treat this meeting the same as a horrible night months earlier. I'll forget this ever happened."

****

A pile of newspapers stacked off to the side of Zerelda's metal-frame bed in the cell looked close to spilling over.

Most of the women spent hours shredding the paper into widths of about five inches and as long as the paper was tall—sometimes close to thirty inches. After taking their time rolling up the paper lengthwise hoping it wouldn't rip, they'd secure the slips of paper from unraveling by wetting the ends with spit and pressing down. They'd store the rolls off to the side in easy reach after using the honey pot.

By the end of each day, urine and feces mixed with the wilted off-white paper and newsprint made for an ugly brown slop. Most women threw an extra scrap of newspaper over the top of the mess before toting their bucket to a cistern located outside at the edge of the courtyard, where they'd spend time walking in circles. She'd heard all their waste ended up in a farmer's honey truck to be spread out over growing fields. She heard a lot but chose to believe little.

As far as the pile of papers dropped off to her cell

each week, she'd read every word before making rolls for later use. Most of the news kept her apprised of happenings around the state. To her delight, though, she'd recently been given a stack containing a few issues of *The Cedartown Review*. The dates were sometimes a month apart, but she appreciated seeing familiar names within the pages. She'd find some comfort in describing Mr. Navarro's kindness to Wondrous or laughing with her over some of the editor's gossipy articles. One such blurb even had him relating a late-night visit to the outhouse after eating too much of his wife's blackberry pie. They'd also giggle over the audacity of grifters stealing pants and shirts off of clotheslines in villagers' backyards without anyone ever noticing. Until they went to retrieve the clean, fresh clothes. Other articles reached out farther from the village, and she always hoped to read something of Corey's antics, but the woman must have been keeping a low profile as she nabbed those cheating husbands.

Sometimes an article hitting too close to her own situation caught her attention, and she'd read it word for word. She'd try not to think how misery loves company, but there wasn't much else to consider.

The other day she'd read a couple of pages from an issue two months earlier. Came across a most intriguing article about a young fellow out of Detroit who'd gotten a pardon within weeks of being convicted of swindling a woman out of her property. His actions had broken her to pieces, and now after being condemned of irrational behavior, she'd be spending years in the Ionia Insane Asylum. But no matter, he roamed around free as any other upright citizen, the pardon board of the state setting him loose after a closed chamber session.

The woman became the criminal while the scoundrel could go back to his errant ways absolved at the hands of the court.

Zerelda's thoughts traveled down a dark path the rest of that day of how the court—jury, to be more correct—saw her as guilty when in fact, the offense of verbal abuse for years had broken her. Narcisco's actions had sent them down a slippery slope causing her to lash out in such an uncharacteristic way. None of that was explored, making it appear she'd lashed out at a kind husband. Could it have been argued he reigned Mayhem down on himself?

The mind games of blame and placing fault repeated on a dizzying loop when her thoughts stepped away from survival behind these bars. One minute she'd curse Narcisco for everything right down to a sore hangnail or toe. The next minute she'd swear at the sheer weakness of allowing her life to get so messed up due to lousy choices.

Sometimes when her thoughts were as far away as possible of how bad her life had become, a glint of light sparkling off a blade came to the forefront of sporadic memories. Odd moments. Never certain if a flash of a straight razor held the key to remembering or if too many suggestions tricked her from recalling that night with any accuracy. She'd wait for more to show itself.

As the cells settled into a murky darkness with a single bulb of weak lighting, she sank down onto the bed and ran a finger over the date of the November 1907, issue—the month of her trial and sentencing.

The irony flared before her that she'd be the one to get such an issue when there were at least twenty-nine other women available to wipe themselves with such sordid news. *Mayhem Trial...*caught her attention...*Ends Today.* This article appeared in letter form to the editor. It was clearly focused on Zerelda's guilt even before the final judgment. She searched for the writer's name—no signature. Only the single letter of "L." Lousy editor with not even enough courage to show the readers who penned such drivel.

...her statuesque continence and beauty a pleasure to enjoy as she set up house and home for her new husband...

He'd said *statuesque* when they met.

...how does she show her gratitude of those early days...

He'd spoken of women needing to get back to caring for their families. The author of the article had cursed her for the inconvenience of those on the jury and having to get back to home and hearth.

...by committing Mayhem...

He'd claimed her innocence, speaking out of both sides of his mouth.

...this reporter has attended every minute of the trial of Zerelda Lena Boronza and finds her guilty of the crime of Mayhem...

He wrote of being present at the trial every day.

...she presents herself like a Queen and we her subjects...

...the jury is prepared to give their decision...

A decision he claimed came with assurances of parole or time served.

No signature—Zerelda wordlessly curled words around her tongue. *Spectator? Reporter? But these are words portrayed how an artist would paint—exclaiming me to be a beauty and referring to me as statuesque. He claimed to be nothing more than one of the jurors.* She'd imagined him with facial hair hiding his strong cheekbones and cleft chin. But his blue eyes proved to be the final giveaway. Did this make him an opportunist? Find a way to get on the jury to help render her guilt, thus creating a sensation in the newspaper, and then come to the prison for a follow-up story? Keep the juicy details going. All the time, inventing a façade during the trial or one afterward, depending on his goal.

He had no right to report and comment in the local newspaper when jurors were instructed—no, demanded—to keep their silence until the trial had ended. This published editorial came out just before her day of reckoning.

The front page of the newspaper fell from her hands to her lap. His spoken words had sounded so kind, and yet his written words so vicious. He taunted her in his gall to write such a letter. And oh, how she'd been hoodwinked.

Her thoughts spun from boiled sugar to cotton candy burning to a crisp black of anguish.

In one swift motion, she stood straight up from the edge of the cot, bent at the waist clutching her stomach, and heaved the meager remains of dinner into the pot. It was a gag so intense bile gushed from her lips, landing atop the grayish mush. She remained stooped over, staring at the mess now representing what had become of her life.

A rancid odor enveloped her head like a swarm of flies the second she swiped a sleeve across her sweaty face. Tears dripped to the floor and puddled in the mush. A moment later, the lights over the catwalk flickered and went out, plunging her and the paper into blessed darkness.

She dared not move as the putrid smell continued to assail her senses.

Chapter Nineteen

April of 1908, Worth a Try

*Every woman in this prison claims her innocence,
but none so loud as the quiet ones.*

*They are the ones who spend their time sitting in
their cells with their gaze following my every movement
as I pass by the bars. Their unspoken words hang in the
air like an invisible fog for fear of torture. They stay
quiet because of punishments of the head iron
tightening at their temples or receiving half a dozen
lashes with the leather bat, or having a meal taken
away. They are the ones I wonder the most about.*

*One woman in particular confounds me. She has
asked upon a couple occasions for a favor of me. I may
have to listen more to her request. If for no other
reason so that she doesn't become one of the crazier
ones behind these walls. Even if what she wants may
cause a ruckus with all the others.*

~Warden Pervis, April 4, 1908

****

Zerelda became convinced more than ever of
moving forward with her idea to help the lost and weary
women in the Jackson prison. A necessity to raise up
the downtrodden and give them a few moments of
attention. Mr. Louis Lewski had opened her eyes to an
ugly fact. Evil came in all shapes and sizes. Narcisco

had proven to be pure evil by twisting every nuance of their struggles against her. Women, such as Corey Strayer, had to fight against a world owned by men. And now, a man with kind eyes and an earnest smile tugged at her senses. He'd admitted there'd been no choice but to let her languish in prison based on the belief of another man's word. Judge Shields had prejudiced the case against her.

But was this Louie Lewski who he claimed to be? He'd disguised himself as a friend when in fact, a wolf in sheep's clothing would have been more recognizable. He'd written an editorial to convict her yet claimed he believed her innocent. Had he not spoken certain words to her face while giving an opinion behind her back? Double-speak. He proved ambiguous, evasive enough to confuse, or deceived her outright. Throw her off the track of his viciousness by showing kindness and concern now. Words spilling out each side of his mouth, trying to fool everyone.

Evil. Pure and simple.

She held her breath as thoughts bounced back and forth, causing her eyesight to blur, and creating a sensation of her head hovering far above her shoulders. Her imitated faint at the beginning of the trial proved to be somewhat convincing, but by succumbing now, she'd end up prone on a dirty floor in a dimly-lit cell. No one would find her for hours reprising the night when she'd passed out covered in blood to be found by Ella the next morning. Her faulty memory still haunted her for an inability to retrieve those lost moments.

"Zerrie," a whisper weaved into her thoughts. "You over there?"

"Am here Wondrous," she replied. "How are you

this morning?"

"Scared."

"Me too. I'm always a bit afraid. Don't ignore those feelings because it'll keep you vigilant in here."

"Remember more stories to help me?"

Zerelda had been so focused on her conversation last night with the unexpected visitor she'd slept in random snatches. Tossing and turning. Not even the braids under the mattress offered up enough comfort to relax.

"Can't think of any right now. How about you tell me a story?"

The early-morning quiet changed to rustlings, groans, and shufflings coming from the cells on each side and across from them. The still air held a musky odor over the prison as rancid as a moth-eaten blanket. No way to tell if the sun glowed as a giant orange ball in the east or started the day obscured by thick clouds. Until release from their cages and allowed to make their way to breakfast and maybe a few minutes in the courtyard, they played a guessing game. The last few outings were cold and crisp, showing signs of the slow arrival of spring. She reveled in filling her lungs with fresh, unfettered air before being hustled back to her cell.

Zerelda ground another hatch mark hidden below the plane of the bedframe showing this as her one hundred and forty-eighth day behind bars. She tucked the nail back into the hem of her dress but not before looking at the tip. The blunt end had sharpened to a point. The unintended consequence of her stay had become a honed weapon. Dust rose up from her graying dress as it brushed along the floor. Her nose twitched, tickled her senses, and then she sneezed.

"Did you place your hand o'er your mouth? Hope so else your soul might escape and I think you might be the only good person here in this place."

"Wondrous," Zerelda replied as she snuffled a second tickle away. "A bit of dust. You and my Babcia would have gotten along. Two halves of a whole. She used to say those same words to me all the time. That old saying must have prevented us sneezing all over everyone. Am I right?"

"Been trying to think of a story, but I can't think of anything else but why I'm here," the young gal continued. "You know Wondrous isn't my true name."

"Figured."

"I've been arrested three times but nothing as bad as the last time. They didn't care a thing about my name, so I told 'em Wondrous. The judge kept smilin' through the whole trial and laughed when he tol' me to get used to looking through bars for a good long eight years."

"What did you do?"

"They called me guilty of larceny," she answered. "I don't even know what that means 'cept I know what I did." Indignation danced around the edge of each word, but she paused as the quiet surrounding them held its breath for more. With a whisper, "All's I know is a diamond ring is waitin' for me when I get outta here. It's owed me. Helpin' someone so's I had to do somethin' for this man. He said as long as I kept my mouth shut 'bout him being involved, he'd give me this ring soon as I get out. He claimed thievery, but he promised me he's hidin' it for now."

"Wondrous," Zerelda broke in. "Help me

understand. You did something bad enough to be sentenced to eight years here, and in due time, you get a diamond ring for your trouble? How do you know the ring will be waiting for you?"

"I have to believe," she answered but didn't offer up any more information.

"And you trust he'll be waiting at the prison gate when you get released?"

No answer.

In the silence between them, Zerelda replayed last night's conversation with Louie Lewski. The sketch the man had presented as an introduction brought to mind the box camera she and Narcisco had used to take pictures of each other. They'd shipped off the unexposed film to be processed and then found themselves checking at the post office every day hoping the pictures had arrived. Her own image had been captured less times than could be counted on one hand—her and Narcisco's wedding being one of those—but she knew the difference. Photographs tended to have a blurry dreamy quality, whereas his sketch had well-defined thin and precise lines.

New photographs now existed from her standing while the prison photographer had her pose two ways. Would she ever see the end results? Everything had happened so fast. She'd been told to face straight at the camera and upon command turn ninety degrees so the flash of the bulb caught her profile. Each time holding a board in front of her chest with her appointed prisoner number of 22701, the fact she was a female, her name and age, conviction and sentence, her accommodations over the next few years, and the date. All etched forever in her mind. Three flashes of the bulb ended any hope of being a Gibson Girl. Her dreams grew as fuzzy as photographs.

She'd been allowed to wear her traveling bonnet still pinned to her massive bouffant of hair for the full-on pose. When it was time for the profile photograph, the bonnet was set aside, yet her hair remained glorious. That was the last time it shone such a deep auburn. She'd smirked at the camera to mask hollowness under her eyes, to deflect the firm set of her lips preventing their quivering, and to dissociate her thoughts from the current untenable situation. She'd pretended of being any other woman walking down a city street on a nice summer day and stopping for the sheer decadence of recording the moment with a photograph.

Her thoughts came crashing back to the dreary day behind bars. Maybe today she needed to press for a conversation with the warden. And to enquire of getting a word to her visitor of yesterday. As sure as she'd be spending more days in this hellhole, a plan began to take shape. Even if her skin crawled at the thought of being in the same room with such a traitor. But now was she proving to be as gullible by the mere fact she was even thinking about him?

"Boronza." Her name came as if from on high. She knew it was echoing down the walkway from some flunky. She looked up from her lap, where her gaze had been unfocused during her musings. Her cracked fingernails and rough skin on the backs of her hands came into view and she cringed.

"Yes," she answered and stood up. She stepped the couple feet to the bars and stuck out one arm similar to last night. Only a few of the other women were ambitious enough to join in with the tomfoolery. "I'm here."

"You've got a visitor."

To Zerelda's surprise, the boots clattering on the walkway belonged to Warden Pervis as he approached her cell, halting mere inches from the bars separating him from her.

He cleared his throat. "Same as last night."

Well, at least she'd be prepared this time. Time to use him for her own purposes. Her Babcia's advice reminded Zerelda she'd get more bees using honey over vinegar. Oh, she'd be laying on the sweetness as thick as possible as long as more sour bile didn't slog up from her stomach.

****

"Thank...thank...you...for seeing me, Mrs. Boronza." Louie sank to stuttering as soon as she walked through the same glassless door. "I hesitated coming, not sure you'd agree to see me."

"And why pray tell, might you query my reticence? Do you suspect my attitude has something to do with you putting me here in the first place?" Well, maybe a bit of mockery before laying on the honey. She declined to let him know of her reading his editorial after their meeting last night. She'd save such a juicy tidbit for another time. "But putting aside my feelings," she said, pausing while the warden moved away from the doorway, "let's discuss redemption."

Mr. Lewski tilted his head in a quizzical manner. His reaction pushed her off-balance, but Zerelda smiled and looked toward him with coyness—the same as she'd done to attract Narcisco—to get what she hoped for. Curiosity also played a part as to why he kept showing up.

Let your smile change the world, don't let the world change your smile. Thoughts of Babcia helped, but tears threatened her confidence. Narcisco may have wondered if she'd used him to pursue the chance of being a *party girl*—a Gibson girl. Why not exploit this man to get what she wanted now? Even if the mere sight of him raised hackles on her nerves no less than an animal's instinctive reaction toward menace.

"I have a proposal for you," she said through a tight jaw and gritted teeth.

Louie's smile broadened, clearly unaware how her whole body grated against speaking to him. He believed redemption was at hand. Even after him being the deciding vote for her incarceration.

"Anything," he responded with urgency, "anything you need, I will do."

"Go back to the moment you convicted me."

"What if I stole H.G. Wells' time travel machine and went back in time to correct this?" Louie smiled toward her with sad, regretful eyes as he shook his head.

"All right, maybe two things I need to ask," she replied, ignoring his attempt at humor. Fearful the moment swayed toward his side, and she'd be persuaded to forgive him brought her back to the business at hand. "Can you please contact two people? My friend, private investigator Corey Strayer in Lansing, and my attorney, Mr. Cruickshank. I'm sure you remember who both of those people are, seeing as you sat through the entire trial. We'll begin with such a task. Secondly, the other is to help me by speaking with Warden Pervis about photographing the women here."

"The first I can do. Do you want them to come

here, or am I to ask them something?" Having a purpose brightened his face. "The second one has me a bit confused. Aren't the women's pictures taken when they arrive?"

"They are."

"Why ask for more?"

"I have an idea. These women need something, and I believe this might help."

Within a few minutes, her words tumbled out of her mouth of how she'd been making loose braids from frayed and used-up fabric, of turning these into bonnets after getting hold of plain hat forms and additional material and strands of ribbon, and of how she wanted to have pictures taken of each convict in this sorry prison to bring a moment of beauty to their lives. He never looked away during her entire rambling soliloquy. He kept bobbing his head in agreement as his smile grew wider the more she expanded on her idea.

"Same as the hat you wore the first day," he said as soon as she paused to take a breath. "The one rolling across the courtroom floor like a snowball in winter."

"When I fainted."

"Did you?" He added a bit of a chuckle at the end of his question.

"Did I what?"

"Faint."

Curious how observant he proved. Zerelda's heart beat faster upon being met with approval instead of disdain. She half-expected complete derision from this man, especially after reading his editorial. The man in front of her—with all of his enthusiasm—didn't quite jive with the person she pictured writing such scathing words. Left her feeling a bit befuddled.

169

Narcisco had always dismissed her ability to create bonnets of note. Hats women craved to own. As much as she despised standing in the same room as a man party to her conviction, Mr. Louis Lewski had managed to gain a measure of her tolerance. Yet she'd hold her opinion, waiting to see if he found success to make something, anything, happen.

****

The women's prison has been in good order throughout. And yet I had the oddest request today and now believe I will honor the wish. As I walked behind one of the women—of whom I wrote about the other night—on her way to see an early-morning visitor, she spoke of dignity among the prisoners. In all my years, few have shown such poise, but her argument was well-spoken, and I found myself listening with a deeper ear.

After she met with the visitor who seemed to rankle her and yet put a certain light in her eyes, the man also took me aside and presented me with a request to allow this woman to help others in a most unusual way. I will consider this.

~Warden Pervis, April 2, 1908

Chapter Twenty

April of 1908, Minutes of Promise

"Ever heard…" Wondrous started speaking but suffered a fit of gagging, sputtering, and having to clear her throat by coughing a few times.

"You all right? Choking again?"

"Yes…yes," she stammered while trying to answer Zerelda's questions. "If three people are photographed at the same time in the same picture, the one in the middle will die first. Did you know?" Wondrous' curiosity of Zerelda's visitor and his intentions had her in on the scheme.

"My Babcia used to say the same. Pretty sure she believed all those superstitions—I might too."

"You take my picture? I want to be all by myself."

"Maybe you're more superstitious than me." Zerelda had curled her feet under her dress, scooting around so the braids under her mattress created a nest. For the first time since walking through the gates, unnerved by the harsh clang of the iron bars rattling against their frames, hope had greeted her with the ringing of the morning bell.

"At least you could have sneezed earlier," Zerelda whispered to her friend. "Remember we need to tell each other all's well or else how can we help? One sneeze, we are okay, but two, we need help."

They were waiting to be released for the breakfast meal if one chose to call the morning serving as such. They were served oatmeal gruel and a chunk of stale bread for weekday fare. Sometimes on a Saturday or Sunday, they'd be doled out a single slice of tough pork rind. Not much better than she used to make for her and Narcisco, but at least she had a choice when precious pennies added fresh eggs as a possibility. Mr. Navarro's smiling face greeted her those rare times she stood in front of the meat counter. She knew he reduced the price for her, and she'd ask after his family to stay in conversation a little longer. Her mouth watered at the memory of good food but soon crushed back to reality by the bellow of the morning watchman demanding the women stand at each cell doorway. Get ready to walk single file to the mess hall or miss out on even the worst morsel.

The guard made his way down the walk, pausing nearly nose-to-nose in front of Zerelda as she stood waiting. His hot stale breath reeked of rye mash as he gave her a toothy grin. She found a spot on the floor to direct her gaze.

"Heard tell you lookin' for a little comfort in this place," he muttered. He inserted the skeleton key into the lock yet lingered before twisting it to release her.

Whispers among some of the women of lecherous guards had left her and Wondrous wary of men moving by their cells. It wasn't enough they had to keep on alert of the crazy convicts—their threats as empty as the coal bin in spring—now there were rumors of rape happening within these walls. As the lines filled up more space, this morning's notch of days she bore emphasized the seeming eternity before being released.

"Well get along," the man said louder, "unless you're not wantin' to avail yourself of our fine food service." His sniggering speech blew a new cloud of rancid fumes in her direction. As if he'd been feasting on rotten meat.

"'oney you goin' to get what's comin'," the old woman a few cells away chimed in with her craggy voice. "Makin' the grand ol'warden hisself pretty happy, are ya?"

In less than a day of pendulum swings of a clock, someone had figured out her conviction, and she received the ugly end of brutal comments. She thought of her visitor, Louie Lewski, and tried to rule him out. Maybe Warden Pervis but he always acted as a gentleman, not engaging in gossip. Someone may have overheard a conversation. Or she had figured everything wrong. Thoughts came back to Mr. Lewski. Maybe his snake-charming ways duped her again, and another scathing article would soon expose her as his imagined high-and-mighty sensation.

The whole idea might be for naught if the warden got wind of disgruntled women—those feeling their crimes were less spectacular and thus one-upped by Zerelda—as well as resistance from the guards. The ones intimidated by her actions. She wished now she'd impressed upon her visitor to act with haste in visiting Corey Strayer and Mr. Cruickshank. She had no way to contact anyone.

"Move 'long." The guard gave Zerelda a slight nudge with his nightstick. The shuffling trudge of the female inmates toward the eating room sent a couple cockroaches scurrying off the grated walkway.

The hem of her dress twisted against her ankles,

causing the nail to catch sideways between her sock-covered legs and the dress fabric.

She raised her gaze long enough to make eye contact with old biddy prisoner 692. Long enough to see a look close to death—the woman's eyes rheumy and watery and clouded with age. As the woman's sight failed, did her imagination ramp up? As one sense diminishes, do other faculties expand? Zerelda turned away. Not out of respect but for fear of what she might become.

"Ain't gonna help any of us here in this place. Jes' leave us be." The woman moved away and sat back down on her mattress, forgoing the breakfast soon to be picked up while shuffling through the line. "I been in here a whole lot of years for more'n what they's think is my crime."

A shiver worked up through her body even as the warmth of the spring morning began heating up the stone building.

"Zerrie? You still ahead of me?"

Wondrous must be having a bad day in the dim light trying to navigate the narrow passageway. The guard separated Wondrous from Zerelda, and she became fearful of drawing attention to them by any show of concern. She faked one sneeze and snuffled with exaggerated loudness, hoping Wondrous got the message they were within arms' length.

"Want to talk, missy?" The guard poked Zerelda's shoulder a second time with the truncheon. "Speak if you got somethin' to say. We don't hold to no secrets."

Chapter Twenty-One

April of 1908, Undesirable in Every Way

Murray is a troublemaker.
For all his enthusiasm and youthfulness, I may have to reconsider his work here at the prison. He has adopted a belligerent attitude toward me when I have cautioned him of using loud, profane, or condescending language. Methinks he is striving to build up a tough reputation with the inmates even if he is relegated to the women's prison.
His tough actions are causing unnecessary hooting and hollering by the women as he walks past them.
~Warden Pervis, April 10, 1908

****

"How 'bout you not turn 'round," the man whispered.

Zerelda didn't dare move, willing her legs not to give out. Putrid air and strains of alcohol mixed in with the sour smell of old meat orbited around her face like a fly seeking a spot to land. She let her arms drop to her sides and stood as still as possible.

"You don't need to scream if you're followin' what I'm sayin.' Ain't no one here to help you."

Nightwatchman Murray, one of the more worrisome guards, had led Zerelda through the labyrinth of basement tunnels on their way to one of the cottages. Half a dozen such places had been built along the outside perimeter of the prison walls. A front door stood as an entrance for visitors, but both inmates tasked with taking care of the cottages as well as those living there could find access through tunnels.

She'd been assigned to clean one of the houses. Her job included taking care of soiled dishes, doing any laundry and ironing, and fluttering a dust rag around the rooms. Waving a rag had always been her best interpretation of dusting. Such a useless endeavor. Nothing heavy-duty by way of cleaning, but she looked forward to occupying her thoughts with mindless chores. Felt close to a reward. She'd been told the day before this coveted position had been deemed hers since there'd been no misconduct since the first day of incarceration. Maybe coveted by many but cleaning up someone else's mess put a slight pall on the privilege.

Zerelda and the guard had emerged through the back door like flowers in spring after walking in the dim tunnel to the cellar-like entrance of the cottage and were now in the kitchen.

He pressed his body in close and snaked an arm around her waist. He pushed his knees into the backs of her legs. She was trapped.

To dream of a lizard is a sign you have a secret enemy. Her Babcia's words never rang so true. Zerelda's nightmares had been full of ugly scale-covered reptiles slithering past her cell door, forked tongues slurping in and around their toothy grins. Awakened sweat-covered and shivering, she'd find reassurance in the darkness alone and isolated in her cell. And now an enemy had her ensnared between his body and the cutting board off to the left side of the wash basin. The Devil had a tight hold of her.

Zerelda shifted away from him, which caused the nail in the hem of her dress to catch on her shoe. If she moved quick enough, maybe she could grab the hemline without removing the spike, jab hard, and hope to find purchase wherever possible. As she slowed any movement, he pushed harder on her backside, preventing a quick decision or escape.

"You act like a queen 'round this prison. Maybe we all need to get down on one knee as you pass by, ya think?"

"No," Zerelda muttered. A ragged scratch came from her throat as her jaw chattered beyond control. She'd gone frozen inside and unable to take any action. "Please, no."

"What do we 'ave here? Beggin' are we. Well, ain't that a grand gesture," he whispered against her hair. Hot breath reached her scalp.

His threat sent a warning chill down her spine. With Narcisco, she always hoped to love away the verbal abuse but never had to deal with physical violence. This guard's intention became clear of him wanting to cause harm.

Her legs wobbled, and a hollow ringing in her ears made her head feel bulbous. Heat coursed its way upward through her body. A real faint sparked lights at the edges of her eyes as her breathing became an erratic pant. Nothing even close to the performance in the courtroom to pull off a fake one as she tried to draw attention to her sorry plight. Panic seared her nerve endings. If she did faint...

The horrendous consequence of blacking out made her head buzz even louder.

"Hey, Zerrie," Wondrous called out. "You here?"

"Wondrous…"

"Zerrie? My eyes ain't workin' so good today but thought I heard your voice. You whisperin' to yourself?"

"Yeah," Zerelda confirmed. "Counting out loud all the work ahead of me today."

Murray slithered his arm snake-line away from her waist, moving methodically backward with unspoken intent. If it weren't for the edge of the counter she'd grasped earlier, Zerelda might have slumped to the floor. With the last bit of remaining restraint, she stood still and waited for this monster to do something, anything.

"We ain't done here," he whispered into Zerelda's hair as he backed away with deliberate slowness so as not to make any noise. He must have already known Wondrous' eyesight grew poor to worse depending on the light source but not aware her vision was at its best in the early-morning hours. Before a full-day's use.

Wondrous moved from the doorway, inching a hand along the wall, never making any indication she knew of anyone else being in the cottage. The guard slipped into the living room area as soundless as an Indian in moccasins. Zerelda reached her hand out toward her friend, and they grabbed hold tight of each other in a hug. Even the smell of their souring once-a-month-washed hair wasn't enough to shorten the hug.

"I knowed someone else was here as soon as I walked through the doorway," Wondrous whispered. "He smelled worse than the rusty ol' whisky still out yonder from my pa's barn."

"How'd you get here?"

"Aw, the warden tol' me you needed my help today so the cleaning wouldn't take so long. He knew I weren't goin' to go anywhere else but feel my way along the tunnel to this house."

"You've been here before?" Zerelda's heart had slowed somewhat, and she kept looking over Wondrous' shoulder, not sure where the guard had disappeared to. He had moved out of her line of sight, and dread prevented her from turning around in case he reappeared.

"Yeah ma'am. Didn't I tell ya they been havin' me scrub the floors of some of the cottages? Figured nothing'd break with me on my hands and knees."

"But the tunnels. They make no sense. Before we'd even walked but a few minutes and made two turns, I knew I'd never find my way back."

"Oh, ain't nothin.' I've been feeling my way along walls forever, so's it's easy to remember what's under my fingers."

Their whispers were no louder than leaves rustling in a soft breeze as they continued to hang onto each other. Wondrous must have taken Zerelda's lead to stay quiet.

"How'd you know not to say anything?"

"Heard something in your voice too. Better to fake my own innocence. I waited for your sneeze. Pretty good, ain't I?"

"So now you're telling me you're quite the actress? How will I know when to believe of your innocence or guilt?" Zerelda questioned her, but instead, they both laughed a nervous twitter.

"So's you ever gonna sneeze?"

Zerelda didn't answer but pressed a finger to

Wondrous' lips to quiet her as they pulled apart from their hug but stood close.

Rusty door hinges creaked, indicating he'd slipped out the front. So now, the moment had passed for them to fear for their safety, but this guard had now fired the first warning shot of more to come. He acted the malicious kind of man, not above intimidation and willing to wait for what he felt others owed him. And he seemed pretty clear on what those payments were.

Zerelda let a tickle work along her nose and gave a raucous loud sneeze as the door clicked shut.

****

"Everline, can you answer a couple of questions?" Zerelda spoke in a soft voice to prisoner number 20463. She didn't want to frighten the poor girl, one who appeared to flinch anytime someone even looked in her direction.

Zerelda had placed a hat atop the inmate's hair after taking a few minutes of piling long tresses already secured in a ponytail. Her hair had been wound in on itself to become a large brown bun. The bonnet sat like deliciously sweet frosting on top of a chocolate cake with strands of fabric braided and tied together to give a fluffed up haphazard mix of bows. Zerelda stepped back, utterly pleased with the final result after laboring over the old tired towels she'd been playing with for months.

"Ma'am," Everline answered, nodding her head the entire time keeping her eyes trained on the floor. "You can ask."

"Why are you here?"

"They say I stole two dresses from a store."

"Did you?"

180

"I took them. Clerk told me to take them home and ask permission of my man to buy them."

"Did you return them?"

"Couldn't. My man tore them to shreds and threw 'em out the window."

"Ladies...ladies." A short, stocky man full of energy and bluster entered the room. He clapped his hands together, mimicking an improbable talent to wrangle some wild animals. "Let's get going on taking these photographs."

Everline shrank back as fear etched across her face.

"It'll be all right." Zerelda placed a hand on the girl's shoulder and gave her a small smile. "We'll talk later. For now, smile for the camera. You look grand with your hair done up and wearing this bonnet."

Helping Everline and then setting her down in front of the photographer, Mr. Jensen, gave Zerelda great satisfaction. Before long, timid prisoner number 20463 had been coaxed into producing a smile that softened her features.

****

"Pearl's my name," the woman pronounced as she sashayed into the room. Her angular face held a haunting look of seduction and sophistication. "Where's the bonnet everyone's talking about?"

"You have your choice," Zerelda spoke up while directing her hand over half a dozen different toppings available for placement on the single platform.

Pearl, prisoner number 22763, new to the prison since Zerelda's arrival months earlier, gazed over the selection. She pointed at the brightest and largest spray of fabric giving its best imitation of a bouquet of feathers and giggled in wicked delight. Even Zerelda had marveled at her own ability while creating the top for the bonnet. Earlier in the week, she'd grudgingly acknowledged some admiration toward Mr. Lewski for delivering some colorful fabric at the permission of the warden. Zerelda worked even harder with renewed vigor as new piece goods slid through her fingertips.

Pearl turned toward the corner where Louie Lewski sat balancing a sketchpad in his lap. "I'll take him too."

Zerelda ignored the comment, although curiosity got the better of her. She sneaked a peek toward Mr. Lewski for his reaction. He kept his stare directed at the sketchpad. The warden had set down a request of her repentant juror upon being convinced this project had value. Mr. Pervis had been shown the sketch of Zerelda and asked Mr. Lewski to draw portraits documenting the inmates in a better light. Hate spiraled around gratefulness like ribbons on a Maypole. One minute, she wanted to throttle the man and the second to hug him for agreeing to the terms. Her emotions never stopped rumbling.

Zerelda worked fast to put the top on the base of the bonnet while they waited for the photographer to show up. Each female inmate lingered and moved slower than when heading to the mess hall, obvious in their intent to be away from their cells for as long as possible.

"Ah, this will be perfect. Don't you think?"

Zerelda nodded as Pearl placed the hat atop her pile of hair, cocked the bonnet sideways, then pulled it down close enough to obscure her left eyebrow. The woman sat on the stool, previously occupied by Everline, and surveyed the small room as if her staff awaited her commands.

"Know why I'm in this place?"

Zerelda shook her head. Gossip gave her some indication, but she wasn't going to admit to anything.

"The judge called me a *common prostitute,* but there's nothing ordinary about me. The newspaper made me sound like the complete opposite of *that lovely Nellie Moon* as they called her. Know who she is? Can't say I do." She rattled on so fast, never taking a breath that Zerelda didn't even try to answer. "Heard they claimed the Moon woman holds all the *grace and poise* for herself, but I do that too. And I know how to make men forget for a few minutes what they have to go home to." She directed a wink toward Mr. Lewski.

Zerelda chose neither to nod in agreement nor shake her head. Instead, she fluffed the feathery fabric and stepped to the side, waiting for Mr. Jensen to return to take Pearl's picture. She resisted another look toward Mr. Lewski for fear of seeing him acknowledging Pearl's intimations.

"Hey, you're a real looker," Pearl whispered as she pulled on Zerelda's sleeve to get her attention. "Ever thought of making a little something on the side with them guards? Some aren't half-bad to look at. Better than most of the men I've been with."

The woman kept talking. Zerelda didn't need to be reminded the guards took what they wanted with no recompense. This Pearl might learn a few hard lessons once she'd been here a while.

Once Mr. Jensen had stepped into the room, the inmate stopped yammering on. He may have heard some of what she'd said as he'd tamped down his earlier enthusiasm and a scowl froze his features.

Pearl remained oblivious to anything but herself.

She perched a bit taller on the stool and gave Mr. Jensen a broad smile and a wink from her right eye. The one still visible with the bonnet tilted the other way.

"Do you want me this way," she proposed, looking straight on, "or how about my profile? I find every angle perfect and lovely. I'm sure you'd agree!"

****

Warden Pervis poked at inmate number 692's shoulder to push her farther into the small room being used by the photographer.

"Can't make me do this," she growled.

The warden ignored her comment. He stood off beside the doorway, placing his hands—which held tight to a truncheon—behind his back. He appeared to be relaxed, but Zerelda knew better by his demeanor. Words slipped throughout the cells he never used the nightstick, although it always put a question mark to his actions as he had a habit of slapping it on one palm. He stood at attention, ready to pounce.

In the last few weeks, since Zerelda's case had been pled to the warden, change came in fits and starts. Even Mr. Pervis seemed different. Talk of closer inspections by the state into the treatment of inmates had brought a few improvements. A small library was filling up with books from local churches, blank books and pencils for writing were available to inmates, and remedial reading classes were held once a week. No one was clear what convinced the warden, but maybe nothing much mattered anymore as long as changes were happening. Cooperating with this project to help the incarcerated women experience a few moments of care and concern might serve as a feather in his own cap upon one of those inspections.

"I'm sorry, but I don't know your name," Zerelda asked in the kindest tone she was able to muster in the presence of possibly the craziest inmate.

No answer. The woman's eyes were flat and blank as she stared back. Zerelda had no idea why this woman had been in the Jackson Prison for at least twenty years, and she didn't need to know. The woman rarely spoke, unlike Pearl, who had chattered on and on of how important she viewed herself.

"Want to know why I'm here?"

The question surprised Zerelda. She didn't answer but instead started pushing a comb through the woman's snarled hair. A gag threatened to erupt, but she held the foul taste in check even though the stale skunky odor worsened with each stroke of the precast comb. Mr. Jensen had brought the latest invention of a Bakelite polymer-molded comb, and although Zerelda knew the substance proved to sometimes be brittle, she still persisted working the tines through this woman's hair. A metal rake might have worked better for untangling years of abuse.

Yet with each stroke, the woman's shoulders relaxed, and an occasional sigh escaped her lips. Fidgeting hands slowed down, leaving the woman to gently massage her fingers in time to the comb strokes. Possibly a buried memory of pleasure from years earlier.

"Have you ever had your picture taken?" Zerelda glanced over at the warden. How much of any of these conversations did he pay attention to?

He appeared engrossed in flicking a piece of lint from the woolen jacket he wore on a regular basis. He raised his eyes as if sensing someone watched him.

Zerelda nodded and gave him a slight smile, not waiting for a response but returning to the task at hand. Doing the bare minimum of helping some women to look tolerable posed a challenge, and she needed to give serious concentration to this particular inmate. The warden had placed this one major condition on her—if Zerelda didn't make each woman appear well-cared for and clean, the project ceased to exist. As well as trying to honor the deal she and the warden had made, Zerelda did start to wonder why some women moldered away in their cell, appearing to have no hope of release. This woman, in particular.

The woman moved her head side to side in a negative answer. Her earlier anger had settled down to a quiet surrender. If answering Zerelda's question might stop this attention, the woman seemed afraid to upset the apple cart.

"Well, if you've never had your picture taken, you might find this pleasing," Zerelda continued. "Every woman here is going to pose wearing one of my bonnets. Help you feel beautiful for a few minutes. Maybe?"

Once again, no answer but now the earlier scowl had relaxed, allowing a few ingrained wrinkles to fall away. Years of vulgarity couldn't erase the old woman of today, but for a brief moment, a show of long-gone youth surfaced. "I got drunk," she whispered. "Just come from Germany and didn't know many words, but I had family here."

"Let's place this one on your head," Zerelda interrupted the woman's explanation. She held the platform in front of the old woman after having placed orange-reddish feathery bows on the top. Zerelda positioned the bonnet upon the freshly-combed hair, tilted the brim forward a bit, and marveled at how the woman's lips curled upward into a shy smile.

"I think my family never knew what happened to me. I couldn't stand upright, so they throwed me into a jail to sleep and then one day brought me here." She looked upward as tears mixed with the ever-constant rheumy-liquid. She startled as she came face-to-face with her own image reflected in a hand mirror. "No one ever came to see me, and I been here over half my life. Ain't never been drunk again, but they won't let me go. Guess I wouldn't know where to go if'n they did."

Zerelda had no answer to offer as the words poured out of this inmate's mouth. She could comment about injustice or how the rules favor men over women or even offer to help plead her story. But she remained quiet while helping inmate number 692 down from the stool and steadied the woman's balance by holding onto one elbow. One of the first realizations the inmates learned upon being surrounded by these stone walls meant each fought their own battles alone. No one else's. This old woman hadn't even had the language to begin the fight for freedom.

Zerelda indicated for the woman to move toward the photographer's area.

"Name's Edith," she whispered. Her voice groaned, rough with emotion. "No one ever listened like you. I want to thank you."

****

"Get what you wanted?" Zerelda cringed at asking Mr. Lewski even a civil noncommittal question. She couldn't resist adding a jab though just the same. "Off to convict more women?"

He stood up from the hardback chair he'd been occupying for the better part of four hours, closed his sketchpad, stretched a bit, and shot a quizzical look toward her. "Beg pardon?"

"Sketching or doing more of your writing?"

"Sorry, Mrs. Boronza, I'm confused."

"Oh, never you mind me," she replied and waved him away like a feral cat.

Mr. Jensen had left the room after gathering up his equipment, and she had but a scant few minutes to rest in peace and feel the warmth seep into her bones before being led back to her dank cold cell. She didn't care to argue with Mr. Lewski, who acted so innocent with his questions and comments yet so devious with his editorials. She'd torn out the article discovered in the old newspaper, smoothed the wrinkles as flat as possible, and kept the vicious words tucked under her mattress with the braids. If ever the urge arose of giving in to liking the man, she'd reaffirm the evil of his thoughts forever printed on paper. How he had nothing more than a rubbery backbone to ingratiate himself to the righteous do-gooders instead of listening to his heart.

...her statuesque countenance and beauty a pleasure to enjoy as she set up house and home for her new husband...

...how does she show her gratitude of those early days...

...by committing Mayhem...

...this reporter has attended every minute of the trial of Zerelda Lena Boronza and finds her guilty of the crime of Mayhem...

...she presents herself like a Queen and we her

subjects...

...the jury is prepared to give their decision...

He turned on his heels and left without another word exchanged between them.

****

"You and me...we're the same."

Zerelda felt certain they were as dissimilar as a sweet little baby duckling and a rattler. Ada Warnier, inmate number 4678, was insane. Crazy as a blind bat with an added dose of viciousness thrown in. Housing her in a padded solitary cell at the Ionia Insane Asylum might be a safer place to tuck this woman away; removed as far as possible from hurting those stuck here in the women's prison.

Even the newest inmate understood how on any given night in this place, something bad could happen. The possibility waited in the corners of the shadowy cells like ghosts ready to haunt after someone stretched their own neck to the breaking point by hanging from an upturned metal bed or of slashing a wrist on their way to a slow death. Some might choose death by one's own hand, but veiled threats of violence whispered down the line of cells struck terror in most. Fear of death by another woman's hand worried more inmates, and this Ada Warnier thrived on adding fuel to the fire.

Ada Warnier's presence amongst thirty women tore at any possible harmony same as adding the devil into a group of angels.

A constant running whisper came from her cell of how she'd do the same as what visited her husband if anyone crossed her path or brought trouble down on her. Sometimes even a look in her direction began an hour-long rant. Many would cover their ears when the

189

woman rattled on mired in her insanity. Her claims ranged from shooting her no-good drunk husband straight through the head because she hated how he looked, of pleading insanity even though she understood every word in the courtroom, and of surviving self-induced starvation until the guards force-fed her milk and stale biscuits. She'd mutter about exacting revenge on one of the guards by stabbing him with a sharpened rung from her cot frame. There'd be hours on end how she'd describe in great detail ways to punish even the smallest slight toward her.

The list went on with as many days in the week, not caring if she had an audience or not. Even the code of silence at night made no difference. She'd whisper as the lights were turned off and go silent for a few minutes as a guard walked by. No one ever guessed of the next rant.

No one knew for certain of the truth either; lies being more abundant than dandelions in an open field. And yet here sat Ada Warnier—a toothy sneer, mousy-faced, soft-spoken female of undetermined age with a heart as cold as a gravestone—comparing herself to Zerelda. She had to have passed twenty years of age, but it seemed more fitting she was going on forty. Other inmates avoided her the same as Zerelda did.

At this moment in time, though, Zerelda didn't have a choice of being here or somewhere else. The other side of the building would have been preferred even if she had to travel one of the darkened tunnels. But when the warden approved this project, he deemed each woman must have her time in front of the camera, and under the explicit condition, Zerelda had to deal with these inmates on a personal level. Ada's turn had arrived to have a bonnet placed upon her head and a photograph taken. Zerelda also was aware Mr. Lewski sketched each inmate by his own interpretation.

"You might as well have killed him, same as me," Ada continued when Zerelda didn't say anything in response to her first comment. "Heard you stepped out on your man."

Zerelda's head whipped around faster than she could stop it. How dare this slovenly woman spread false rumors. Is that what people were saying?

"Heard too you showed him how he weren't no man." Ada was taunting Zerelda after seeing how she'd gotten to her.

Zerelda thought about responding but chose instead to keep words buried deep. This inmate had a way of grasping at every little bit of gossip or rumor floating around the prison, hoping to get an argument started. She'd never spoken to anyone what had happened between her and Narcisco, and she didn't plan on taking this inmate into her confidence. Anything Zerelda said might have given affirmation to the two women being similar. She wasn't having it.

"Ah, Mr. Jensen." Zerelda sighed as the photographer entered the room. "So glad you are here. How soon will you be ready to take pictures?"

"My dear, true art can never be hurried," he replied. He made a grand flourish of moving the heavy drape away from the back of the camera as he added new plates into the apparatus. He looked down at a list of women inmates. Checkmarks had been placed to the left of each name of those already photographed.

By Zerelda's count, two women were left to be dealt with in this small community.

"Now, who do we have here? Are you Ada Warnier?" He looked up from the paper toward the female sitting on the stool.

"You goin' to stare at me all day or get this done?" She defied him with a glare to say more.

Zerelda cringed. Nothing like challenging the one person within these walls to photograph a subject's good side!

Mr. Lewski had settled into his usual spot and appeared to be doing a preliminary outline. When he smiled toward Zerelda, indicating he was ready to continue, he flipped to a new page of his sketchpad.

"Ah, I see we have only two women left to photograph," Mr. Jensen said, indicating Ada and Zerelda with a sweep of his hand. "The two of you."

Zerelda recognized the cue to finish arranging the fabric atop the bonnet on the inmate's head. After making sure the bows were in order, she stepped over to a small table positioned off to the side out of range when the pictures were being taken. The table displayed a riot of fluff with all the different hat toppings.

None of the toppings used on the bonnets for the other inmates held any attraction for her, so overnight, she'd created a fifth choice using a swatch of fabric Mr. Lewski had passed onto her through the warden. To prevent anyone from choosing this crown today, she kept it somewhat hidden under the least used feathered fabric. With this session coming to a close, she slipped the new one out from under the old and spent a little time fluffing and rearranging the bows. The stream of new purple satin woven in and out, over and under would always be in her mind's-eye although lost to the grays and blacks of a completed photograph. The colors probably would all blend together and might not show up as much. She didn't care. This represented her personal prize for completing these moments of beauty in the ugliest place ever to exist. She wanted to be different from the other inmates. This idea had arisen from nothing, and she gained a bit of satisfaction from pulling off such a project. Made up some for how ostracized she'd felt from the world outside over these months.

"Hey," Ada called out. "I want that one." She pointed toward the table while wickedly waggling a bony finger at what Zerelda balanced in her hands. "I want those bows."

"Hold still, miss," Mr. Jensen chastised her. "We are ready for the shot."

"No," the gal yelled. Dust ruffled up from the dirty floor as she moved toward Zerelda, looking like she was going to rip the first bonnet off her head. "I want what she's holding."

Mr. Lewski stood and stepped over to come between Ada Warnier and the table as Zerelda moved more in front of the unique set of bows to hide them again. With her hand holding firm to the table, Mr. Lewski's arm grazed hers as he helped create a wall between the bonnet toppings and Ada Warnier. Human touch, so rare in this cold harsh environment, made Zerelda's skin tingle.

"Sit back down, or I call for the warden." Louis growled out the words, never budging nor saying more.

Ada froze.

All of the women knew Warden Pervis to be fair. But any reason to *call* him might result in being placed in a solitary room, the leather cap strapped to their head and tightened down, causing a headache worse than a night of downing hooch.

For a long second, Ada looked from the table to Mr. Lewski to the photographer before lowering her hand from the hat on her head and taking sluggish steps back to the stool. Zerelda held her breath and waited. After sliding alongside the table toward the chair, Zerelda sat back down, placed her folded hands in her lap, and released panic with a large exhale.

"Get this over with," Ada snarled, glaring toward Zerelda yet looking not quite as intimidating as earlier.

"Thank…" Zerelda began a second before Warden Pervis walked into the room after the guard had escorted Ada Warnier out of the room. She'd stood up from the chair she'd been occupying during this final session and took a step closer to Mr. Lewski. "…you."

Mr. Lewski gave her a quick nod and smile before slipping out of the room. He'd almost looked to say something but appeared to wait for a more opportune time. Just as well.

The article she'd come across in the newspaper continued to burn in her thoughts. Anytime this man appeared to be weaseling into her good graces, she'd pull out the worn piece of paper and remind herself of his complicities. He helped to convict her, believing a judge more interested in closing the case than being fair. And yet she couldn't resist rubbing the spot where his arm had brushed up against her hand. Or thinking how he was ready to protect her.

With each passing hour spent between these walls, as Narcisco walked around free, her resolve strengthened to survive at all costs, same as a soldier in the horrible rigors of battle.

Chapter Twenty-Two

October of 1908, Endless Days

The tunnel seemed darker than Zerelda remembered from previous times. But with Wondrous by her side, they made it without tripping or bumping into walls on their way to the cottage they'd been tasked to clean. Their chores included getting to the right cottage, pulling out the cleaning supplies from a back room, doing their best to make it habitable for the resident guard, and heading back to their cells. Leaving no trace of their hard work except for the freshness of the Borax or baking soda they so liberally made use of. They hoped to be in the cottage at least two hours. Two hours away from their cells.

Two hours they'd usually try to dawdle out to three before being missed since they both reveled in how they could take deep breaths, make noise, and move around freer than any other part of their stay in the prison. They'd find a way to drag it out to five hours if possible.

Sunshine filtered in through curtains tied back to each side. Wanting the room to be as bright as possible, Zerelda walked from the kitchen, through the parlor, and into the front room, pushing heavy drapes aside. Dust motes lit up like tiny stars in the rays blasting through the windows.

"Let's start here in the parlor," Wondrous commented as she poured some Arm and Hammer baking soda from a paper envelope into a steel bucket. She cranked the hand pump a few times before water started trickling out. The pump stood off to the side in the kitchen, with the spout just reaching over the sink edge. A few drops of water had trickled down to the floor. She scooped water from the basin into the bucket and made a thin slurry in order to dampen the cloth they'd use for dusting, wiping down door frames and windowsills, and to glide over knickknacks. "Bedroom next, then leave the kitchen for last before we have to head back."

"Well, ladies, what do we have here?"

Zerelda and Wondrous spun around in tandem like a chorus line of dancers. Nightwatchman Murray leaned against the bedroom doorframe with an ugly smirk spread across his face. A nervous twitch affected his left eye giving away an unpredictable edginess. His clothing was in disarray as if he'd stepped into them while trying to walk; his long underwear halfway buttoned up from his waist, his boots unlaced, and his uniform pants drooping low on his hips. Suspenders dangled around his knees like he'd been unleashed. The two women were speechless, waiting for Murray to make the next move.

"You supposed to be here?"

"Sir," Zerelda spoke, letting derision drip like the leaky hand pump, "this is our day to clean this cottage. Could ask the same of you."

Her attitude did not sit well with Murray. The smirk flattened out as straight as a taut line of string, and his eyes darkened under his bushy eyebrows.

"None of your damn business."

She'd never heard him swear, although always assumed his normal vocabulary would be peppered with every guttural word known.

He pushed away from the doorframe and advanced, coming to a standstill in the middle of the room while his fingers worked the undone buttons of his underwear. He then slipped his arms into the suspenders and snapped them with his thumbs for emphasis. Zerelda and Wondrous cautiously stepped closer to each other hoping safety in numbers would stall but not startle the monster in front of them.

"Keepin' me waitin' ain't helpin' you any…at all," came a gravel-filled hiss from the doorway to the bedroom. Ada Warnier leaned in what she supposed would be a seductive pose. She'd stretched her left hand upward to the top of the doorframe and bowed her body outward to accentuate her figure. Clad only in her wrinkled under-dress, bare feet on the wood floor, and a mass of hair so wild and tangled, she looked to have stood in a whipping wind for an hour. On top of that unruly mess perched one of the prettiest bonnets Zerelda had ever made! She'd never realized it had been nicked from the room where the inmates had been photographed.

Murray whipped around to confront Ada, which gave Zerelda the few seconds she needed to shim up her prison rag just enough to work the nail out from the hem and slip the spike length-wise into her palm. She covered her hand with the towel she'd been using to dust after wrapping her fingers around the nail. The spike felt warm to the touch as if it had come to life in anticipation.

"Get back...get out of here," Murray demanded of Ada. "No one's supposed to be here with me." He then turned back to Zerelda and Wondrous, glowering in their direction and spittle running down his chin as he sputtered, "You keep your traps shut. You hear?"

At that moment, as if on cue to emphasize his words, Ada sailed the bonnet to the floor and then trampled it with both feet. The platform crushed flat as the ribbons splayed outward. She mimicked the smirk Zerelda and Wondrous had first seen on Murray's face. Rage burned upward through Zerelda. Her hand shook with such violence the spike rattled in her palm, ready for battle. She was ready for a fight too.

Murray raised his arms toward the two women. Zerelda's first instinct came in wanting to protect Wondrous, whose eyes grew worse with each passing day. As Murray's left fist came downward, she stepped in front of her friend, and he caught Zerelda in the head. His knuckles landed square between her right temple and eye snapping her head sideways. She stumbled a couple steps away from Wondrous as she tried to maintain her balance. Sight in her eye went black and burned as if a poker had been inserted from the side of her head. The nail in her left palm slid to her fingertips, and she grasped at it before it could clatter to the floor. Another attack felt imminent. Out of the corner of her still functioning right eye, she caught a flash of his other hand heading toward her friend.

With too much to comprehend, time slowed.

In the blink of a second, but seeming longer than an hour, Zerelda lashed out with the nail toward the hand about to reach her friend. A howl echoed through the cottage as nail met hand. The point of the shank tore through skin sinking deep into Murray's opened hand as the fleshy palm received the end with minimal resistance. Merely a slight squish of a response as ligaments and cartilage separated from bone, almost as easy as slicing through a tender cut of pork with a sharp knife. She experienced nothing at that moment. Void of sound, defiance, or feeling.

"Good God, woman," he screamed. "What the hell have you done?" He grabbed at his wrist as blood spurted outward in a chaotic waterspout. Red on the wood floor, spots hitting the fabric furniture, polka dots flying to the curtains, and some even attaching to the ceiling. Blood rained red down on him while his face turned a sickening shade of gray.

Ada screamed and ran back into the bedroom.

In a heartbeat, the frantic inmate had grabbed her clothes and shoes from the bedroom, picked up the trampled bonnet, and ran for the door to go back through the tunnel. She'd be dressing in the near-dark if she was lucky and caught trying to sneak back to her cell if unlucky. Either way, she'd lost her free ride to whatever independence the nightwatchman may have offered.

Wondrous stood quiet and unmoving. Zerelda never took her gaze off Murray and how he kept flipping his hand back and forth. The nail end peeked out at the back of his hand, covered in blood, while the nail head looked polished as ever. Zerelda's habit of stroking the shank at night served as a talisman for her in moments of stress and had put quite a gleam to it. Time stood still and of a halcyon quality, especially now with Ada out of the cottage. Wondrous still had not moved while Zerelda and Murray continued to stare at each other. He glared as he grabbed hold of the nail head and pulled the weapon back through, releasing another torrent of blood and a guttural growl emanating from deep in his throat. He let the nail clatter to the floor. It rolled a couple inches and came to rest in a large puddle of darkening blood not far from his feet. She never looked at his hand but held his gaze with her one working eye and tried to ignore the buzzing in her head. The swelling of her other eyelid continued to balloon out so far her eye had disappeared under blackening skin.

Murray went silent as he grabbed an armchair cover and wrapped the cloth around his hand to quell the bleeding as a tourniquet might help. He turned and walked back into the bedroom, appeared again within a few seconds with his uniform shirt and boots, and proceeded to follow the long-gone Ada through the tunnel door. He spat out parting words, though, as if to bolster an ego wilting faster than a kid having to say he's sorry. "Clean up this place, or you'll be in a mess of trouble." With that, he disappeared.

Seconds of near silence followed, other than long releases of air after heavy intakes of oxygen, and then the world started to spin up again like a Victrola recommencing. A cardinal's whistle could be heard outside the kitchen window singing one of its many tunes as a cloud passed, and the sun seemed to shine brighter than before. Zerelda and Wondrous turned toward each other and hugged, still trying to figure out what just happened in those last ten minutes.

"You be the bravest woman I ever met." Wondrous' voice held awe.

"We've got some mess to clean up," Zerelda

scoffed and waved her hand as if to dismiss what they'd just been through. Once they'd pulled apart, she began assessing how much blood had sprayed throughout the room. The blood had started to congeal in odd-shaped little circles as it got darker. Flashes of the morning Ella woke her from her stupor in the old farmhouse worked through her thoughts.

She kicked at the weapon removing it from a puddle of blood, bent down to retrieve it, then dropped the coated spike into the bucket of baking soda water Wondrous had prepared earlier. It landed with a splash, with the water soon turning a pale shade of pink. She grabbed the nail from the bottom of the bucket, dried it off, and inserted it back into the hem of her dress. Zerelda took the time to lodge it far enough so as not to fall out.

"You okay, Zerrie?" Wondrous moved one hand up alongside Zerelda's face. "Heard that thunk and took me back to when my brother would smack a tree with any stick or log he'd found just to threaten me. I hated him."

"I'll be fine," she replied, dismissing the concern. Time crunched for the possibility of someone coming to look for them. "We need to clean up this mess. Don't move. Let me get more water and towels."

"I can smell the blood," Wondrous said. "Get me a wet towel so I can get busy. You clean up what I can't see or reach."

They worked with diligence bolstered by the hope of avoiding punishment if caught late in their return. No sounds, laughter, or conversation filled the cottage. Fabric being scrubbed against hard surfaces, sloshing water on the floor to mop up the chaos, and the snapping of bed linens as they remade the soiled nest vilified by Murray and Ada were the only sounds. No conversation as they worked hard. Whoever used the cottage—with Zerelda being pretty certain it wasn't nightwatchman Murray's—they never needed to know what had happened on this beautiful sunny day.

They wandered through the small cottage double-checking for anything they might have missed. The parlor, front room, and bedroom appeared unused. The kitchen—with all the blood scrubbed away—needed a bit more attention. Zerelda put a couple pots up on a high shelf and brushed off a couple crumbs from the worktable. As she turned back toward the large basin to check the hand pump no longer dripped, her arm brushed against a small salt cellar made of glass with decorative metal scrolling around the top rim. The miniature spoon popped out of the salt spreading white grains on the worktable.

If you spill salt, throw a little over your left shoulder. The Devil balances on your left shoulder, your Guardian Angel on your right. Blind the Devil, so he can't take your soul. Her grandmother's words rang loud and clear in her head. She'd tossed salt over her left shoulder too many times to count, hoping to save her own soul. Now this ritual felt more important than ever before. Zerelda gathered up as much of the spilled salt, placed her back to the basin, and tossed the grains with a slight flourish to release them. The crystals started to dissolve the second they hit the little bit of water remaining in the basin. She breathed a sigh of relief.

Before long, the two of them linked together arm-in-arm to head back through the tunnel to their own hellhole, trying to erase what had happened. Hoping the Devil never followed.

Zerelda knew the slap across her face would sting for quite some time as it turned black and purple, then a sickish green before yellow. But she felt secure in how they'd hidden their part in this debacle. She pressed fingers to her temple to gauge the swelling and felt alarm at how her eye still had trouble focusing as an incessant throb beat faster than her heart.

Chapter Twenty-Three

November of 1908, Gifts

An old woman confounded me for years. I looked up the reason she had been confined to our walls. Or, as many still say, gone to the tamaracks. Such information is always at my disposal, but I first try to get to know the women without prejudice.

She spent her time behind these steel bars not long after the day when this prison was nothing more than a log cabin. Today she died, and we had to bundle her up in a woolen blanket and carry her out of the prison. No family, no ceremony, no recognition; just another nameless plot dug alongside the cottages. Soon to be forgotten.

My history weighs heavy on me tonight as I contemplate all the years I've been here. Of all the men and women having been housed here. Our chaplain has suggested more projects, as this one with the bonnets might help. Let the inmates express themselves through art, poetry, writing, or anything creative. I may even suggest to him we interview each and every one. Let them tell their story. I may find a way to help those who merit saving.

But how can I sit in judgment of anyone and decide if one inmate is more important than another.

~Warden H. Pervis, November 5, 1908

****

Pervis laid the pencil down on the desk and folded the cover up and over the pages of the journal. A slight crinkling came off the stiff paper. His thoughts weren't so much on how to save these poor souls, caged by their own misdoings, but more on his own preservation. If dissecting his feelings served any purpose.

With each inmate—the females in particular—he lost a bit more of himself questioning the souls of human beings. He had watched too many of them fight for survival, never knowing if they won or not, witnessed women behind bars struggling for some form of dignity only to fail, and wondered once too often if this place even helped society. To be held captive like a wild animal instead of nourished and cared for. Most are left to travel down the dark road of thoughts to never find some form of redemption. Thrown away.

A couple years back, the woman who just passed had given him a gift of a small leather strap. It had half a dozen holes punched along one side to hang keys. She'd fashioned small rings made from bits of wire from the bed frames. Each hole had a metal ring to hold a single key. The key holder had remained in his office, hanging across from his desk as a reminder of what a smile can do.

She was one of the sourest looking women with lips forever turned downward, dark eyes shrouded by sagging eyelids, and mottled skin peppered with pockmarks. Day after day, the mattress on the steel frame sagged to fit her form as she stared toward the catwalk, never speaking to anyone as they passed by. Including him. One day they happened to make eye contact, both holding on a little bit longer as if the other didn't want to sever the connection. He allowed the slightest smile to cross his features. She looked away.

The next day they did the same. The day after, more looks. After another week, she'd offered up a curl of her lips. Nothing much more happened until one day, a few months down the road, she held up one finger like a traffic cop, and he stopped. She stood up from the bedding and reached out her left hand with her fingers curled around something. He wondered if something had gotten stuck in her grip and needed help to remove it. Her hands always looked to be in a permanent cramp with fingers curled inward, dried and cracked fingernails, and blue veins running across the back of her fists like a thousand rivers. He marveled the bones hadn't cracked in two with her hands shattering on the cement floor into a dusty heap. She turned the one fist over and unfurled stiff fingers as if any movement brought pain. The leather strap rested in her palm. She never said a word, yet she kept looking down at the piece in her hand and back up at him, encouraging him with her eyes to accept this gift. He did so after reaching one hand through the bars. She turned back toward the bed, shuffled a couple steps, and resumed her position as before.

"Thank you," the warden said, not sure what he held, yet knowing something unusual had happened.

"Keys," she whispered.

Had she spoken, or had the single word come from another cell? He waited.

"For your best keys," she uttered.

"Why?"

"You smiled." Her answer came in a thin voice as old as the wind. "No one else ever took the time."

He found himself at a loss for words. He waited. But she'd finished and thus took up her vigil of bowing her head down to look at old hands as they rested as still as death atop the graying dress.

Yesterday morning as he walked the catwalk, he pondered what few words he might say to the old woman as he had so many mornings before. A simple *hello, good morning,* or *did sleep come?* If an effort made any difference. As he approached the cell, the air hung heavy and silent. The sight before him lay as peaceful as anything he'd ever witnessed inside these cold walls.

She'd settled flat on her back, her head propped up by her few meager pieces of clothing piled on the pillow, her hands clasped as if in prayer, eyes closed, and the slightest of smiles gracing her wrinkled face. Evidenced by the pale gray hue edging her cheeks, she'd been gone for a few hours.

His thoughts still centered on the old woman, but he started comparing the similarities found with the *bonnet lady* as he thought of Zerelda. She reminded him so much of the one recently passed and wondered many times if her fate would be similar. Zerelda had become even quieter over the last month. He'd taken note of how she now bent her head down whenever he walked by as if to hide something. The light may be playing tricks on him, but he thought once he noticed shades of purple, green, and yellow descending down her cheek. He felt a certain kindness toward her and had wanted to ask, but she'd turned her back to him before he spoke.

Yet even now, he'd remained convinced the smallest kindness could make a difference. With him acknowledging the old woman, he had shown compassion during her final days. Something she may have never known in her lifetime. To this day the leather strap held only a single key. The one for her cell. Locks had been changed, and old keys no longer needed, but this one remained.

He mused if Zerelda might well follow in his same steps. The moments of care she gave female inmates of combing their hair and placing a bonnet atop may have been what some needed to survive another day in this prison. One may never know how or if a moment makes a difference in a life but friendliness and understanding never hurt.

****

PostScript. Maybe a change is coming. Old inmates die, new ones arrive, and some are rewarded. Rumor has it our younger inmate has an overzealous lawyer, and he's looking for a way to discredit her court case. Is reversal possible? Is that how some of these women will be saved?

And yet I question if this system will ever change. One female inmate has become ever more surly as she sits in her cell, whispering of every injustice she's suffered while I find myself having to recruit a new nightwatchman. For no apparent reason other than one has disappeared from duty.

Possibly I have overstayed my worthiness. But here I am, becoming a maudlin old man. Best be getting on my rounds.

Chapter Twenty-Four

May of 1909, Time Travels On

Zerelda walked into the visitor room.

The last time she'd been down this path, Mr. Louis Lewski filled the room with his nervousness. Admittedly, some good had come from meeting him but not enough to make her life better. Some nights she'd look at the editorial, but many times before lights out she'd ignore the newspapers. As a single initial for the writer's name sat at the end of the scurrilous article, she continued to suspect him. And now, he kept trying to cover his tracks with kindness.

Today's visitor came as a surprise, though.

The sight before her consisted of a tall woman decked from head to toe in a floor-length leather coat, boots gracing her large feet, and a bonnet on her head held in place with a scarf extending at least six feet long. She'd tied the lightweight fabric under her chin and created a large bow with lengthy ties to float about her as wispy as butterflies. As a broad smile lit Corey's face, Zerelda felt a punch in her stomach of how well-put together and beautiful her friend looked. Especially compared to how she must look.

Before Zerelda said a word, Ella stepped out from behind Corey and cowered as intense as a timid rabbit readying to bolt. Her dark eyes blackened even more as fear appeared to root her slight figure to the spot.

"Ella…Corey…I cannot believe my eyes!"

Corey moved to the side, so her companion stood in full view. Ella's hair puffed out as delightful as a spent dandelion, as if one more gust of wind could scatter the curls to the sky. This gave Zerelda pause of what might have happened.

"Ma'am," Ella whispered. "Is you okay?"

A long table separated Zerelda from her friends—the same table where Mr. L. Lewski had spread out the drawing before her. Ella started to make a move to come around the table, but Zerelda put her hand up.

"No, we cannot hug, otherwise you will be asked to leave. Please, please let's sit down," she said, pulling out the hardback chair from the table and then taking a seat across from them. "Oh, I can't believe you are here."

"We'd have come sooner, but some arrangements had to be finished up first," Corey spoke before taking a seat. She didn't wait for questions but continued, "I bought an autymobile! Some call them automobiles but I like *auty* better. Sometimes we go faster than a horse's gallop!"

Zerelda looked from one friend to the other.

"And you drove here?"

Corey then did the most feminine gesture Zerelda had ever seen in this woman she'd known for such a short time but knew they were destined to be life-long friends. Corey twirled around to show off how the long coat—with slits up the sides, partway up center back, and two shorter slits at the hemline of the front—fanned out. The scarf skimmed along the leather fabric, twisting to her twirl.

"You look better than a Maypole—a glorious, beautiful spring pole," Zerelda exclaimed to Corey. She then turned to focus attention on her diminutive friend. "And, Ella, how are you? Would you look...oh my, your hair is so different."

"Oh, ma'am, my hair ain't no different," she replied as she raised both hands to her head. Surprise sparkled in her eyes. With a frantic look spread across her face, she patted at the wiry black curls.

"The wind." Corey giggled, beaming as excited as a kid with a new a toy. "I am now a part of the mass revolution—as the newspapers are calling it—by buying an autymobile. And, I can now go faster than a horse could ever pull a wagon!" "

"She picked me right up in front of Mrs. Barnerd's house. Tooted that fancy horn and near woke up every dog all 'round us," Ella joined in. "But oh, ma'am, there's nothin' same as riding with Miss Corey drivin'. We bumped along like a stone skipping down a hill as dust blew up behind us more'n I could ever clean up in my whole life. And oh, the wind. Never had so much blowin' on my face less'n I'm standing on a hill right before a storm."

"But we had fun," Corey stated. She raised an eyebrow toward Ella to see if more would be added. "Am I right?" Ella swallowed hard, nodded, and stretched a grin so wide even her molars were showing.

The three of them sat in silence for a split second. Zerelda felt a warmth of happiness for the first time in forever. She hoped Ella realized the autymobile wasn't going to be the death of her—at least today—and Corey's expression shone with the knowledge she'd done the best possible kindness for her two friends.

****

"Just as planned," Corey began her tale once they'd settled down and stopped talking about their conveyance. "Not too long ago, someone left a box just inside my office door."

Zerelda thought back to the small vestibule she'd stepped into a lifetime ago that set the stage for a horrible outcome. She'd pushed the ball rolling down the hill, gathering up an oily straight razor to come between her and Narcisco's powers of will. Life had changed, never to be the same. Years piled one upon another of grievances, arguments, and stubborn behavior where a nasty outcome now proved inevitable. When her breaking point came crashing down on him, their marriage dissolved. Narcisco's verbal abuse made up part of his nature and Zerelda being left behind for another woman grew larger than life in its ugliness. Why did it still come as a surprise she sat in a prison?

Something far less gruesome than this crime of Mayhem could have landed her in prison—like the mere threat of injury—especially the way women were treated. An inmate such as Edith falling down drunk and waking up in a local jail resulted in a cruel incarceration no man would suffer. He'd have been congratulated for the sheer talent of waking up and then having the wherewithal to stand while still in the lockup!

Her memory still faltered with erratic behavior. She'd suffer glimpses of her and Narcisco grappling with the straight razor, then nothing but timelessness black until Ella's frantic urgings the next morning. Zerelda moved her head back and forth to rid her of unwanted thoughts or maybe to shake something loose from her memories.

"A box?"

"Full of money. Three thousand dollars, to be exact." Nothing more needed to be said. Payment ensured her silence. Corey had been brutally honest regarding these anonymous gifts left at her doorstep. "And now I am the proud owner of my own transportation."

"Any guess where the money came from?"

"Oh, I'll tell you another time," Corey answered Zerelda's question. Coy as ever about divulging too much information. "We're here for another reason."

"You don't hate me, do you?" Ella blurted out her question before Corey continued.

"How could I hate you, Ella?" Zerelda implored. "You tried so hard to help me. Even digging out some of Narcisco's cleaner clothes for me to wear to make that escape on a bicycle. I must have looked the fool. Laughable, in fact, thinking I could get away as if nothing ever happened."

"No more discussion," Corey spoke up in a let's-get-back-to-business voice. "We've been in front of the Michigan Supreme Court at the state capitol building regarding your case."

"You and Ella?" Zerelda interrupted at such an incredulous statement.

"No, not her and I," Corey replied, waving her hand between the two across from Zerelda. "Mr. Cruickshank to be exact."

Zerelda's thoughts started spinning like a cyclone ripping across the land, changing up history in the blink of a whipping wind. Mr. Cruickshank must have something solid to be allowed to even get in the front door of such an imposing stone structure in Lansing. The façade of the building alone, combined with massive columns and a grand staircase leading to the twelve-foot wooden doors, intimidated even the strongest-willed person. It would scare her even more.

"He's compiled a whole laundry list of reasons to get your case dismissed," Corey continued since Zerelda had gone dead silent. "Think back to the trial if you can. Witnesses were questioned out of order between both sides, with the judge allowing witnesses back for one question here and there. The judge sat three women on the jury, which has never happened this side of the Mississippi. One of the worst grievances came when the judge inserted his opinion to the jurors of treading light on your sentence swaying the jury to bring the trial to a quicker end. And a most disheartening article. Oh wait, you may not know about the article."

"I know about it," she answered. "Nearly used that page of newspaper after you-know-what. Didn't, though. But have given serious thought to using it after each time I read those awful words."

Ella giggled then covered her mouth with her hand.

"Well, Mr. Cruickshank suspects someone who attended the trial each day wrote the article trying to influence the jury. The editor has chosen to not give up a name. Maybe a juror wrote the article. He's hoping the Supreme Court will force the issue. If none of that works, I'll make this whole *fopdoodle* of a case go away." Corey paused as Zerelda fingered the skin along her right eye socket. "Are you okay?"

Zerelda had developed a nervous habit over the last six months—as if her hand had a mind of its own—of fingering where the bruise used to be anytime something rattled her. She'd wondered if the thunk of rock-hard knuckles had become her moment when nothing could get worse. Her personal epiphany. She had become capable of doing anything to save herself. A moment worth remembering to not black out as she had with Narcisco but to treat each struggle with clarity. Her quick action saved herself and Wondrous convincing them both of no more backing down.

"I'm fine. A bit stunned to tell you the truth about this turn of events. Sitting behind these stone walls going on two years, one tends to forget there's a whole world of people going about their daily lives with their thoughts centered on their own existence. Women having babies, farmers working in the fields, shopkeepers helping others, some are happy while some are not, or that anyone even remembers me."

Corey reached across the table. Zerelda brought her fingertips to within an inch of Corey's hand. Ella stretched forward the same. The three sat looking back and forth at each other short of touching fingertips as a quiet resolve moved into their eyes of this bad situation turning around. Thoughts of maybe someday linking their arms together and walking free, unfettered by their own personal prisons. Zerelda snorted out a short laugh followed by Corey's higher-pitched delight and Ella's sweet giggle. Their glee settled back down, and they sat in silence, smiling at each other.

"You know I used to think about loving the abuse out of Narcisco. That if I treated him nice enough, he'd change. Now I know offering my love and gratitude to the wrong people goes unrecognized. Or should I say, to the undeserving."

Chapter Twenty-Five

August of 1909, Day of Dread and Joy

Tomorrow is the day I've either looked forward to or dreaded. They both feel the same to me. One of our most cooperative and gentile prisoners will be leaving today. Her release makes me happy and hopeful a better life awaits her. Dread comes from not having a chance to talk with her or see how she interacts with all the prisoners. How she might further help inmates as she did with the bonnets.

She has kept to herself and rarely found a reason to complain while waiting with apparent patience for her emancipation more than any before her. I sincerely wish I could have been the one to grant her a quicker release from this life.

With her now leaving, what does that say about me? Do I continue working in this hellhole in the hope of helping someone—anyone—willing to listen? Do I become a grocer as my erstwhile wife kept suggesting until her last dying breath? To exist without this lot in life. Time will help my decision become clear. And with my heartfelt wish, if I get word of her flourishing outside these walls, maybe I will find courage to do the same.

~Warden Pervis, August 6, 1909

****

The document to the right of his journal caught Pervis' attention. When the courier had brought the packet a week earlier, he knew the contents. The unopened package had sat on his desk for a day before he slid the pewter letter opener along the top edge. The slit had gaped open as wide as a whale's mouth. He wondered if Pandora's box of feelings might overwhelm him; good news for one but hard to swallow for another. Bad news crushing fragile emotions as bad as icicles spiking into a snowbank.

The former was the case. The Michigan Supreme Court ruled to release Zerelda Lena Boronza from his prison for reasons he had memorized after reading over the list too numerous to count. And the day had now arrived.

The People v. Zerelda Lena Boronza

Lack of proper procedure during court appearances—Arrest on suspicion—Circumstantial evidence not conclusive—Outlawry of prosecution—Amicus curiae.

A trial necessarily must follow set procedure.

An arrest made on suspicion cannot retain suspect more than two days without evidence.

Guilt must be based on conclusive evidence not circumstantial.

A judge circumventing the law to influence a decision.

Volunteers of the female sect are not allowed to sit on a jury, acting in amicus curiae, as a favor to the court.

Error to Livingston. (Shields, T.W.)

Mayhem. Respondent was convicted. Reversed.

Attorney General Frederick S. Michael, for the

People, confessed error.

Boronza, Zerelda L., Respondent, having been convicted of Mayhem and sentenced to five years' imprisonment now brings error. The Attorney General, on careful consideration of the case, has concluded he cannot uphold the conviction. We are of the same opinion. But inasmuch as we are to consider whether the prisoner needs be retained for further trial or discharged, we are compelled to deal with it far enough to determine that question.

Respondent is charged with wreaking Mayhem on one Narcisco Boronza on the Seventeenth day of September, 1907. The complaint and warrant for her arrest were made two days later, the Nineteenth of September, 1907. The testimony showed fervor ran rampant with a trial date set so quick impartial jurists could not be found and were also exposed to theatrics during the trial in the form of Mr. Boronza's performance.

Without going over all the facts, an outline of the principal matters will be enough to explain our legal views. Sometime during the night of September 17, 1907, a drunken Narcisco returned to his home after threatening his wife with violence earlier in the day and proceeded to stumble to his bed. It appears they struggled and she may have inflicted injurious harm on Mr. Boronza. Harm that could not be reinstated, only a gaping wound healed. The next morning Mr. Boronza was discovered at the Cedartown firehouse. Mrs. Boronza had gone missing. She was not found for questioning until two days later when one Zerelda Lena Boronza was discovered in the late afternoon wearing men's clothing and riding an ill-working bicycle eastward out of the village. The authorities arrested her. Narcisco Boronza had reported to the fire department, where he served as the fire chief, and wished for his wife to be arrested for the harm she inflicted.

The proof of blood on Mr. Boronza or of Mrs. Boronza leaving the village is of improper importance and does not warrant by any honest and well-founded supposition of her complicity in this crime. Including the fact no weapon was found. This verdict was decided on mere speculation and circumstantial evidence.

From the facts as detailed by Attorney Cruickshank, we stand unanimous and in firm belief he made out a case of justifiable defense on Zerelda Boronza's behalf to protect herself from harm by leaving her home and hearth with her husband under the threat of bodily harm. But whether this could have been shown in exacting measure or not, the case needed to be put before a proper jury consisting of men only upon this hypothesis. If they thought she had acted out of fear for her own life, the respondent should have been acquitted on those grounds.

This, however, is now immaterial because even if the act of Mayhem was voluntary, there can be no doubt that having been provoked by implied violence and the lack of display of a weapon, the crime could not be more than self-defense; and therefore tried in error.

With the conviction erroneous, the judgment must be vacated. And inasmuch as if the respondent had been indicted with a lesser charge, the prosecution would have been outlawed. She should have not been subjected to a trial. Inasmuch as the Attorney General has appeared in this case, we can pay no attention to

*suggestions from other parties, and as we know, with
no doubt, the papers before us are correct, it would not
be fair or just to postpone the decision.*

The other Justices concurred.

The last few words blurred under Warden Pervis'
gaze. She'd been pardoned by the highest court in the
state. Maybe not judged to be of complete innocence
but vindicated of the malicious charge leveled upon her.
Getting too old and sentimental for this job. He pulled
the discolored handkerchief from his uniform pocket to
swipe his face and blow his nose. *Such an old fool I'm
becoming.*

****

Zerelda paused with the gate at her back, facing the
old stone building. A white butterfly flitted around her
shoulders. *If the first butterfly you see in the spring is
white, good luck will come your way all year.* She
hoped Babcia's words were never truer.

She had taken a tentative step toward the spot
where her freedom began two feet beyond the opening
so the gates could swing closed. Her legs shook but
worked quicker as she approached the end of the
walkway. She'd walked alongside Warden Pervis. He'd
been more than gracious to carry her single valise
containing a couple of books, the coat she had worn a
year and a half earlier, the bonnet she'd held onto upon
arrival, the damning article published during the trial,
and the sketch Louie had given her. Plus, the nail which
had given her security and she'd kept sewn into the hem
of her prison dress. She now wore the simple dress
from the day she and Wondrous came by train but had
stuffed the gray prison rag into the honey pot.

They both stopped short of the gate and turned in

tandem as if they'd practiced dance steps. They nodded tentative smiles toward each other in a solemnity befitting the moment. He then headed back to his life behind the bars while she turned to walk through the gate.

Within a few short heartbeats, she stood on open ground. The wrought-iron fence separated her from the warden where he stood inside the walls of the Jackson State Prison. Zerelda turned to offer another nod and smile to the one man who had offered compassion and kindness. Warden H. Pervis faced her standing securely behind an entrance serving either as his choice of employment or his own prison, and he gave a short wave.

The warmth of sunshine beat down on her shoulders, and a slight cloud of dust kicked up from her worn boots as she toed the land where freedom surrounded her as fragile as a bubble about to burst. Liberty had a smell—unfettered abandon to experience the warm mustiness blowing off her clothes, the crunch of rich dirt below her thin boots, and the wind bringing the sweet smell of clover from an open field.

How she'd taken for granted a life without physical bars. Invisible boundaries had confined her in a life where verbal abuse left her incapable of doing even the most mundane task without fear of criticism. She'd adapted to that imprisonment and came close to accepting a lot in life never envisioned. Now no one would ever take control over her own movement and choices.

Never again would she dismiss her Babcia's advice. No matter how vague. For now, she tenderly filled her lungs with the sweet scent of freedom and relished these moments of peace. Those fateful words put to her a few days before her wedding to Narcisco came to mind. If she'd only taken the message to heart and listened to what her Babcia tried to tell her. How choices made by her would become Narcisco's to decide. She released the air from her lungs and let go of her past.

She turned to greet the people in her life she'd forever treasure and never take for granted. Corey stood with a lopsided grin on her face and another spectacular hat perched on her head. Brilliant shades of purple and crisper fabric, so the bows stood firm in the breeze. This bonnet surpassed in beauty the one Zerelda had given her as well as the one Corey wore during a visit, and Zerelda was thrilled her friend had found her own style.

Mr. Cruickshank rustled one hand around in his briefcase, looking to make sure nothing was amiss before they drove away. He held the document freeing her. She'd take a closer look later. Maybe someday.

Ella stood between the two of them. Her wide smile spoke volumes as tears coursed down her cheeks.

And Louie. He continued to be a bit of a mystery to her. The one person she might be willing to explore a bit further now that they would be able to spend time together without a chaperone. He never gave up on her even if he had been bamboozled during the trial; maybe there could be forgiveness. Maybe someday.

"Don't be shy." Corey laughed as she gathered Zerelda into a loving embrace.

Ella grabbed hold by wrapping her arms as far around the two of them as they'd go. "We can now do more than reach fingers toward each other! And now, let's head home."

Home…how had she not considered what she'd do tomorrow or the next day? Where she would end up living to start a new life as a free woman. Narcisco? What of him? They had no proper marriage. Moving back into his house might be a necessary evil if she couldn't come up with anything else. Maybe disappearing was the best option. Her kneecaps began to shake up and down, as an endless pit of indecision pushed at her confidence. She looked at her friends, knowing full well they could never understand the despair working through her or of her inability to make any kind of choice.

Home and a bed…maybe Corey would take her in for a bit. Ella helped with the Barnerd household, but she lived as poor as a church mouse, treasuring any scraps thrown her way. Mr. Cruickshank and Mr. Lewski stood beaming at Zerelda, but they were oblivious of her situation. They'd no doubt trip over each other, offering up advice if asked but falling into another trap of being dependent on a man soured in her mouth.

"Come stay with me for a few days," Corey spoke up. "We've got so much to figure out of where you'll live, what you can do, getting you some new clothes, and letting me bring you up to snuff on all you've missed."

Relief traveled through her body like a stream trickling into a still serene lake. The poetic feeling was such a new sensation her whole body calmed and made her legs go a bit weak.

The men's smiling faces dimmed to slight frowns—either from thinking they had another solution or realizing they hadn't been of any help to begin with—as Zerelda nodded toward Corey. Zerelda grabbed up her single valise and marched toward Corey's autymobile before anyone offered up something different. Zerelda, Ella, and Corey climbed aboard, leaving the two men to head back in the other vehicle. Mr. Lewski took the lead by turning on his heels and headed for the driver's side while Mr. Cruickshank struggled to open the passenger door.

A quick crank on the engine, loud clattering, gear engaged, and a plume of dust. Zerelda never looked back as they drove away from a place that failed to crush her spirit. Her only regret being Wondrous didn't occupy the seat next to her.

Chapter Twenty-Six

August of 1909, All in the Drink

Zerelda didn't need to wonder about still being married to Narcisco.

On the day of her release, his sorry life came to an end. The irony was never lost on her of how her story began again while his hubris failed him—hooch wouldn't kill him, he'd always said. Well, maybe the drink didn't kill him directly but falling off the viaduct to land headfirst at the entrance to the tunnel where Zerelda and her Babcia used to sing at the top of their lungs felt like justice in its purest form. Maybe on his way down to the intractable ground, the echoes of long-ago songs wormed into his pickled brain—*these are Grandma's glasses, this is Grandma's hat, this is how she claps her hands and lays them in her lap.* Zerelda clapped once in solemn celebration then placed her quietening hands on her lap as she listened to Corey's news report. She'd settled into a guest room in her friend's beautiful Victorian home until decisions could be made. Corey's home in Lansing was located about a block north of the building housing her investigative services office.

Two days had passed, and now her old life lay buried beneath odd circumstances setting her free to chart her own path. In fact, Corey had a continuous stream of good news, even if some seemed a bit harsh by reveling in someone else's demise. Narcisco had no other living family, so she inherited the parcel of land, a partially reconstructed mill, Ol'Sam, and a house nearly too scary to go back to. She imagined razing the house for all the vermin he may have accommodated during her time of incarceration. She'd be instructing Mr. Cruickshank to sell off everything except for good Ol'Sam. Unless he could locate a kind farmer to allow the horse to enjoy a green pasture and live out its days in peace. If the attorney wasn't up for the task, maybe Ol'Sam would end up within the Lansing city limits in Corey's postage-stamp-sized backyard.

"And now the best part. " Corey kept breaking into Zerelda's thoughts as they'd wander away from all the updates. "How I got the money for my autymobile. I can't tell anyone, shouldn't even tell you, but…"

Zerelda looked up. "Are you sure you want to tell me?" Corey held more secrets than most, so she waited without saying more while Zerelda made the decision of whether to hear more or not.

"I used to believe ignorance kept me in bliss, but these last few years have proved otherwise," Corey replied. "Yes. You need to know this, and I won't be breaking any confidences. But you do need to promise me one thing."

Zerelda raised her fingers to her right temple, beginning to wonder if this habit portended bad news from this point forward. A slight throbbing inevitably developed whenever she recalled how the swelling took forever to go down, being able to focus her eye taking even longer, and how a tender spot about the size of a penny never changed from the sallow yellow back to her skin tone. The bruise had become a permanent fixture. She raised her eyebrows in Corey's direction, indicating she was ready for whatever promise Corey alluded to.

"Narcisco gave me that money to keep me quiet. Once I found out what he had, I nailed him dead-to-rights of his guilt."

"My Narcisco? No not mine. You mean someone else. Such a skin-flint never admitted to anything more than two coins to rub together after he squandered so much."

"Oh, he had the money. I'm not sure, though, how long he had been hiding the money in the mill. Maybe the money didn't even belong to him. Maybe he had earned it and kept it hidden for if he decided to leave." Corey moved closer to Zerelda, sat down beside her, and took the now-jittering hands in her own. "It was probably all stolen money, but we'll never know for absolute now that he's dead."

This is almost more than I can bear, but I need to know. She closed her eyes and whispered, "Tell me everything."

"In a nutshell, he had been stealing money from the fire department since long before your mill burned. The books he kept showed one figure, he'd then subtract what he thought was due him, and he kept a second set of books to be viewed by anyone interested. The amounts were never very much at any one time, so no one suspected a thing. Until Josef James—you remember him at your trial who wanted to say more, but Narcisco's attorney stopped him from speaking? He came to me after you were convicted."

"Corey, my head is spinning. Why am I only now

finding out about this?"

"All in due time, my dear. Lots of scheming and conniving had to work on my part, but we had to find out the truth in its entirety before making a move."

"Narcisco was a sly one," Zerelda confirmed. "If he'd had any inkling you were onto something, you'd have never found out."

"I haven't even gotten to the best part. Here goes. Josef and I came up with a plan to see if we could get Narcisco to talk. And, if so, hide a witness or two to hear everything. Not as difficult as we thought as most everyone at the fire department suspected foul play but had been afraid to speak up. According to anyone I spoke with, Narcisco always implied he had some kind of dirt on each person, and he'd freely—and with great glee—turn it into gossip and rumors. You know people don't care if there's truth or not in the story as long as it's juicier than a ripe melon."

"…more Devil than man…" Zerelda interjected, a little deflated how little she knew about her dead husband.

"To say the least, he played off of everyone's weaknesses," Corey confirmed, then stopped. "I'm sorry how those words sounded. I don't think you were weak, but maybe naïve and more trusting than some. Anyhow to continue. One afternoon, I dropped off a note at the firehouse requesting a meeting with Narcisco for a few hours later. I didn't know if he'd see through my wanting to meet with him alone, being a single woman in town with no attachments. But he took the bait. Sorry about being so forward, but he seemed to think all the ladies were ready to fall for him. Such a *cox-comb*! I got my reply back through Josef as he came around about an hour later, indicating Narcisco wanted very much to sit down to talk. The meeting had been set for six o'clock. I arrived at the front door at six-fifteen. He looked to have grabbed up his coat, making to leave when I walked through the door. He laughed, spreading a cloud of moonshine vapors or whatever soured his breath as if he had started drinking hours earlier. He even swayed a bit when he turned around to invite me in."

"He wasn't a happy drunk, and that makes me afraid for you trying to trap him. But sounds like he also had to rise to some challenge he saw in you. He might have been like the Narcisco I knew when we first met. On some kind of good behavior," Zerelda added.

"Exactly as I had planned—keep him guessing. Josef and his brother, Anton, snuck in the back door to wait and listen in on the conversation. Which, by the way, did you know Josef and Anton are cousins to your friend Mr. Navarro? I think your favorite grocer might also have helped Josef realize he had done you an injustice by not speaking up earlier."

Zerelda's head throbbed, bringing her close to wit's end. So many perceptions were changing in such a short time. She took a couple deep breaths and indicated for Corey to continue with the story.

"I played on the fact Narcisco might have convinced himself I'd been swayed by his looks...sorry...since he kept speaking of loneliness," Corey continued. "He had a table set up with two glasses and a half-gone bottle of rye mash next to them, and a single lightbulb flickered at the front of the firehouse. Dusk had set in, which worked to my advantage as I'm not sure how I'd have reacted if he started making advances. I obscured my face in the shadows as he seemed to do the same. He sat, I sat. He took a long swig from the bottle before pouring the remaining into the two glasses. Heaven knows drinking that swill is against my religion! I go for only the best aperitifs. I encouraged him to finish it off."

"You were playing a dangerous game being there," Zerelda said. "I wish you hadn't."

"I'm glad I did. Mr. Cruickshank fought with the Supreme Court to what seemed a dead-end. I had this proof but wanted more than anything to keep it hidden and use it as a last resort. Looking to get something, anything, out of Narcisco to prove you are a better person. Then the court might take favor on us. As it turned out, we didn't need any of this proof once Mr. Cruickshank pleaded to the court other more substantive reasons. But we hit pay dirt that night more than we'd ever thought possible. Between you, me, Josef and Anton, and Mr. Cruickshank, no one else knows anything about the money. Narcisco became so drunk his boastfulness brought on his downfall. He rambled on about the stupidity of the men working for him. About how trusting they were of him. About how he persuaded them to start rebuilding the mill based on him preventing false rumors or gossip from spreading through the village. About how they'd pay him for his silence out of gratitude. There were moments his ramblings contradicted his own words."

"But where did the money go? And you? How did you come into so much money?"

"Nothing illegal on my part, I can assure you. Once Narcisco had passed out, Josef, Anton, and I found the two sets of books and figured out how much money the old sot had been stashing away. We even found his stash! In an envelope taped to the bottom side of a drawer. So, all of the money has been returned, and Mr. Cruickshank helped me destroy the false set of books. Proof of his wrongdoing doesn't exist. Josef and Anton are thankful to be free of Narcisco as well."

"Still doesn't explain how you ended up with so much money."

"Ah, my persuasive attitude. The next morning—before dawn and before anyone was moving around in the village—I pounded on the firehouse front door and woke up Narcisco. We had a second conversation, just him and me. I told him what had happened last night, how we rectified the problem, and how nothing would come to light. Including how Josef and Anton would encourage all of the men to help rebuild the mill. Getting him to agree to leaving the men alone and stepping down as fire chief was a hard sell, but he agreed. He went from being so hungover with a glaze in his eyes to practically doing a jig around the room. He recognized the gift I offered of him not having to sit in prison. But he still had me to contend with. I didn't care whether or not he went to prison, drank himself to death, or walked away. He found out I wasn't giving up. And how I could make his life easier by keeping this information to myself for a fee. Three thousand dollars, to be exact. Oh, the shade of mottled red his face became!" Corey stopped, stood up, and walked a few steps as if there was a way to put distance between her and the ugliness of playing such games.

Zerelda joined her to stretch cramping legs and to process all of what had happened. "But Narcisco doesn't...didn't...have that kind of money," she said.

"We were living crop-to-crop and what he processed at the mill."

"You dear, trusting friend," Corey replied with a shake of her head. "Josef had found a stash of money in the mill after that fire caused partial damage, and they were cleaning up the mess. By Josef's estimate, the bag contained more than three thousand dollars. Narcisco had stuffed it into a steel oat barrel of Ol' Sam's hidden behind the unburned stall. Josef told me about finding the money, no doubt something you knew nothing about, and told me he didn't dare touch it because it belonged to you and Narcisco."

"Three thousand dollars?"

Yes," Corey replied to Zerelda. "Take a deep breath, because there's a lot more. I informed Narcisco the price for my silence matched that same amount telling him three thousand dollars. I gave him less than four hours to get it to me, or I'd be marching right down to the sheriff's office. I may have been overconfident, but I took a chance and boarded the train back to Lansing."

Zerelda had been standing but now slumped into the nearest chair. She covered her face with both hands and mumbled, "Is there more?"

"Oh, yes. My plan worked—maybe my reputation preceded me, or his attorney had spilled the beans. That *hawkshaw* probably couldn't keep his mouth shut even to his own detriment. Narcisco didn't question the amount or my silence. With a few minutes to spare going on four hours, that box was placed in the vestibule of my office. He might have even been on the same train and followed me there to see where to deliver it. I'll never know and don't care."

Corey paused to take a drink of water.

"He must have been petrified of being found out," she then continued. "I suspect the bag in the barrel may have contained more than my asking price, but I'm not greedy."

"Oh, Corey, this is unbelievable but so very credible. All I can do is shake my head and say thank you."

"Remember how I said the man always has to pay for my silence? Consider the portion of the hidden money as payment for my services," Corey smiled, "especially since you'll no doubt gain a nice sum from what's left in that barrel plus by selling everything. Please tell me we are heading there to clean out the mill and your belongings, the sooner the better."

Before Zerelda formed an answer, the chimes at the front door sang throughout the house.

"Oh dear, I have a bit more to tell you but let's wait," Corey warbled out, doing a quick skip toward the entrance.

Mr. Louis Lewski. He came into the parlor with his hat in hand and a shy smile on his face.

"I sold one of the sketches," Mr. Lewski started right in even before they were all settled in the parlor, "except for the one I gave you, to a collector. Made a tidy little sum."

"Well, aren't you successful," Zerelda responded, trying hard but failing to keep sarcasm out of her tone. Success came to him on the back of her trouble. Would have been gracious of him to ask first since this all happened because of her.

"I wanted to ask you first," he replied with an urgency that surprised her. "I had to move as quickly as possible and had no way of knowing where you were. I may have been a little bit of a dullard thinking this through as I came to the realization going back to Cedartown and Narcisco wouldn't be your choice. And now I hear he has died. My condolences…"

Zerelda shot him a look of disdain. "You come here two days after Narcisco falls to his death and think I want your condolences? Have you no decency? Have you no shame? The article?"

"Article?" Louie's voice went up a notch.

"Wait, Zerelda," Corey interjected, "you've got this all wrong. I still need to tell you more. Mr. Lewski did not write that article."

"Article?" He continued acting about as bad as if he'd missed an important second act of a play.

"The article you wrote of how I needed to be punished to the highest for the crime of Mayhem. Something I can't even say with absolute certainty actually happened." Zerelda jumped to her feet, ready to escort this man from the house and her life.

"Zerelda, please listen," Corey pleaded. She took hold of Zerelda's hand and tugged her back to the chair she had been sitting in. She turned to Louie and said, "Would you mind leaving for about an hour? I need to tell Zerelda a couple more things, and it is very urgent she know these before more incriminations are made."

****

"He's left," Corey said, coming back into the parlor after ushering Mr. Lewski out. "He's going to walk around a few blocks but will be returning. Persistent if nothing else."

"Let's get this over with." Zerelda sighed. She couldn't imagine one more thing she needed to hear, but Corey was equally persistent. A headache had crept around the edges of her eyes, and she began to think the quicker she acquiesced, the sooner she'd escape to go lie down and digest everything. Maybe get some true and deep sleep knowing Narcisco never again posed a threat to her.

"Two stories, and I'll make it quick. When Narcisco had lost all sensibilities, moments before he passed out in the firehouse, he also made two admissions. His voice was so slurred both times I had to ask him to tell me again. The story never changed, so I believe everything said to be true. First off, he wrote the article. Narcisco wrote that damning article, asked the newspaper not to put his name at the end under some convoluted sense of blackmail to the editor, and put an "L" as the initial because he claimed—and these were his words—he's *such a great lover*! He wanted some initials to show at the end, such as I.I. or L.L., to keep readers guessing, but the editor chose not to go so far in the deception. Mr. Cruickshank pressed the editor for an answer with no luck on whether Narcisco was the one to write the article. But I'm certain we can believe the word of a drunk man unloading all his sins."

"Humph," Zerelda muttered. She'd blamed Louie for writing the article, certain he had penned it by his mere attendance every day during the trial. But Narcisco, and Corey, and Ella, her attorney, and a whole courtroom of spectators showed up every day too. The list was endless. She never thought Narcisco could be so vengeful, but then a revered appendage had been removed, and he must have felt the sting of impotency during the trial. "The second thing?"

"Yes, the second one. Not quite as pretty.

According to our fool—your now-dead husband—he fessed up he wasn't as drunk as he acted the evening you threatened him with a straight razor. Yes, he stated to having a bit more than his usual, but he admitted to being completely aware of you from the moment you stepped into the bedroom. He saw the glint of a blade but never imagined anything more than a threatening notion and definitely not of the harm you might inflict. At the point you and he were at loggerheads holding the weapon with as much strength as you both mustered, he played the odds. His exact words—he *played the odds*. If he overpowered you, he feared he'd harm you. If he let his hand go limp, he figured he'd get a nick in the gut but nothing more. The odds were against him, though not realizing the strong woman you had become working the majority of the chores around that place. When his hand went limp, between the strength and the weight of your body behind the weapon, the blade cut through his long underwear and found something even softer and more malleable. He witnessed his most important appendage being separated from his body no more difficult than lobbing off a healthy chunk of watermelon."

"That's what he thought of at the precise moment he began to bleed? Watermelon?"

"Well," Corey continued, "he confessed to being somewhat drunk, and in his telling of the last thing he thought of was bright red juice." Corey couldn't help smiling at the comparison. Zerelda smiled back, and before long, they were both laughing.

"Red watermelon? Blood? He didn't just play a fool, he was," Zerelda said between giggles as a rush of relief swept through, knowing the slicing wasn't all of her doing. Both she and Narcisco were both complicit. The thought sobered her, and she muttered how they both were, "playing the odds."

"He did also tell me he did love you at one time."

"But no longer," Zerelda replied. "That was another lifetime, different people."

****

The conversation had been stilted. Zerelda had no idea what to say to Mr. Lewski once he had returned. He wasn't perfect, but he wasn't the villain who wrote the article. He had always been a gentleman, coming to the prison when everyone else seemed to have forgotten her, being the go-between to help the female inmates with photographing them wearing unique bonnets, and he had done all with utmost sincerity. She'd never know if any of these women's lives changed because of a few minutes, but she may have been saved by Mr. Lewski's persistence. Maybe more than she cared to acknowledge.

He'd gotten requests from interested parties to show additional sketches of her as well as the other women as word spread across the state and even into other parts of the country. They'd become a bit mythical as the woman who wore a hat in prison, of the man who sat in the corner and sketched each female inmate, and of the emotions found in those miniature pieces of artwork. He also spoke of how a newspaper editor from out-of-state pestered him on a monthly basis for the right to print the sketches in future editions. But Mr. Lewski had different ideas.

"The second original sketch—you have the first— bought by the collector amounted to more money than I've seen in a whole year," he had told Zerelda. "If each drawing fetched as much as that first sale, I—maybe we—will be set for life," he said with a rise of an eyebrow in question.

"We?"

"These sketches are because of you. What right do I have of benefiting without including you?"

Zerelda tried to keep her features as neutral as possible but for the first time in her life she felt cared for—second only to her dear Babcia. As if maybe, someone needed her for who she was. Not to clean house or work her fingers raw or to be an imaginary Gibson Girl on his arm being paraded around no better than a show horse, but someone who saw value in her being. A person worthy of getting to know better and to be a partner with. The prospect scared her more than anything else in her life—even counting being threatened in the prison or by Narcisco. A veil started to lift inside, and she allowed a shy smile in return for his compliments.

"Can we talk more over a dinner downtown?"

"Well, Mr. Lewski," she crooned. "You seem awful forward in assuming I am available."

"Oh, Zerelda," Corey piped in. "Stop playing coy and go enjoy a meal. It is almost 1910, and after all, we are modern women. Women like us don't need chaperones!"

Chapter Twenty-Seven

Spring of 1937

How the years have disappeared...

Zerelda's thoughts made her hands pause. She held the poof over the powder she'd been using to dab her face hoping to fill in some of the wrinkles starting to resemble a road map with no destination. Twenty-seven years had passed since that fateful day in Corey's house, listening to all her friend had found out.

She passed her fingers over the yellowish circle at her temple, always remembering to press a little extra powder to the spot. She didn't want to explain. Not that anyone ever asked, but she remained wary. She'd taken to wearing her hair on the bobbed side instead of long to be able to flounce her graying hair around her face. Helped to hide the spot as well. Though the days of being a Gibson Girl had long passed, memories persisted of some of those heady times full of glamour. Her life had settled into a comfortable quietness she craved, filled with beauty and style.

The reflection of her hands in the vanity mirror wavered with a slight constant shake. An annoying tremor had started about a year ago, particularly prevalent whenever her schedule included entertaining or socializing. Her hands never again looked anything but soft and well-manicured. Never again to suffer harsh cleaning or hard work. They had become her prized possessions this last quarter century.

She and Louie had planned a quiet twenty-sixth anniversary after the previous year's magnificent quarter-century celebration, but they'd been thrown for a curve. He had died nearly a year ago, leaving her with a modest fortune and a few unsold original sketches if ever the need arose. Even as his health slowed him down—stomach ailments that never seemed to subside—he had sketched morning to evening. The times he would pause, set down his pencil or piece of charcoal, came during their afternoon tea ritual. Their conversation sometimes touched on times before their lives came together but more about how the current state of world and national news might affect them. Never was there a dull tone to their bantering.

She now had a catalog of sketches of how she looked at varying stages of life and at least one charcoal drawing of her in prison wearing the hat no other inmate wore. Hers alone to stand out from the rest during that project. None of the sketches were ever as revered as the ones he drew during the trial and then the bonnet experiment, but every single sketch brought in extra money. The demand had never truly ceased.

He'd had a way of catching the slightest emotion within those drawings as grays and blacks combined over stellar white paper. Whether it be happiness, a contemplative look, serenity, a reflective attitude, or even sometimes sadness, his work showed passion. For every sketch, they'd attached an adjective as the title. A few years ago, a local holiday card company had convinced them to share their artwork through reproductions of some of those most sought-after pieces. The demand for those cards had astounded both of them and assured monetary security.

Zerelda missed him, but a part of her had always known she'd be the one left behind. A future of being alone didn't make her uncomfortable but sometimes the silence and emptiness in the big house they built years ago rattled her brain. Once in a while, she could almost hear long-gone female inmates running a cup along the metal bars or whispering a conversation between cells or the rustle of newspaper after someone had used their honey pot. She knew the wind created that imagery from her memories, so she'd wait the moment out or start making plans for the next day.

Over the span of sixty years, she'd never celebrated a birthday more meaningful than this one. Her Babcia would have loved this planned party with more than a simple little cake and a single candle to blow out. She might also have decried Zerelda for the over-abundance on display for this afternoon's party.

Zerelda had no control over the plans and had even been warned to stay away until the appointed time and then sit back and enjoy. Surprise had warmed her heart that someone cared so much. But then her friend never disappointed. She and Corey Strayer had remained life-long friends, living a few blocks from each other in Lansing, and shared many a meal or afternoon tea together. Often a few weeks passed of not seeing each other—in particular when she and Mr. Cruickshank were off on some adventure. They had become partners in the sense of enjoying each other's company. Many in local social circles thought their activities to be scandalous as they traveled together, but they chose to let the gossip slither upward as smoke in a chimney.

The two of them—Mr. Cruickshank more than Corey, it appeared—found delight in hearing of the scandalized gossip. Corey had done so much to change his view of life by experiencing excitement and fun. His stuffed shirt actually had a few wrinkles these days.

She hoped dear Mr. Navarro and his cousins, Josef and Anton, chose to make the trip to Lansing, but she knew they might not come. The few times she had returned to Cedartown, she made a point to see all three of them, but time does steal away friendships. Whether from distance or never finding common ground other than in strife, those bonds can loosen. She'd never forget them.

Ella did not have to work, but she thrived on being useful. A few years after Zerelda and Louie were married in a simple ceremony at the city hall, Ella had come calling. She had taken the train from Cedartown a week after Mrs. Barnerd had passed away. She needed employment. Ella became not only her right-hand helper but also the epitome of a true friend. No matter, day or night, Ella remained steadfast. Zerelda hoped she gave her friend the same gratitude. The strength of their bond proved stronger than blood sisters.

Through Mr. Cruickshank she had heard the disturbing news of the sitting judge during her court case. He'd become completely flummoxed when his proceedings were questioned, and the decision of the jury overturned. Rumor swirled of how Judge Shields had let the moonshine own him, and he took to wandering through the courthouse halls late at night, clad in his official robe, banging his gavel on any solid piece of wood along the walls and staircases, and muttering, "Order, I will have order in this courthouse."

For all she knew, he might still be there. With the year 1937 and upheavals and changes upsetting the whole judicial system, Judge Shields may have overstayed his usefulness. They called the changes *modernizing* but all Mr. Cruickshank spoke about revolved around more paperwork, more meetings, and more ridiculous roadblocks to justice. No wonder he and Corey chose to take more trips.

Someday when the time felt right, she'd ask Mr. Cruickshank of his thoughts about women. He had taken on her trial, worked hard throughout, and never stopped pursuing the inequities dealt by Judge Shields. But…and it still rankled her…he'd referred to her as a "mere woman" during the trial. Or maybe he viewed all women in a similar manner. She chose not to fault him for words used in the heat of the battle, but as she has always found words spoken in haste or anger are quite often the most truthful. At that moment, she might have been his damsel in distress to rescue during the trial. Or did he also view Corey as a "mere woman" who needed an escort in their adventures? Someday she might broach the subject but found it easier to let that go. The bond between him and Corey made Zerelda envious at times yet too precious for her to interfere with.

Narcisco's attorney had blustered his career all the way to the Michigan Supreme Court. Thankfully his appointment occurred long after her case had been overturned by the higher court. She supposed he still sat there, all superior and mighty, and looking for the next moment for some sought-after attention. Curious though, Zerelda wondered if he would have thought twice about throwing up any obstacles to her freedom. Corey had let slip where another box of money had come from after the trial. Mr. Walton's discomfort during the trial with Corey in the witness stand may have been due to keeping his own indiscretions under wraps. He'd bought her silence with a tidy sum of money, and she never failed. Business as usual for Corey.

When Corey broached the subject of the party, Zerelda knew who needed to be invited. Warden Pervis should have been on the list. After his retirement and about five years after she had been released, he'd "found" himself in Lansing and had called upon her. He had aged, shrunken in on himself a bit, and suffered a horrible stoop forward from his waist. He still showed kindness and compassion in every word spoken. He'd presented her with a leather strap to hold one key and told her the story of how the effect a smile could make in another person's life, comparing her bonnet project to the smiles on some of the female inmates when they were being photographed.

If a prison can exude a fond memory, she'd smile thinking of him. She and Louie's conversations about those rough years always ended with the concession there never existed a better warden than Mr. Pervis. Didn't matter he was the only warden they'd ever known.

Quite a few years earlier, he'd been asked to write about his experiences as warden, and he'd offered up his nightly journal entries acknowledging at the beginning of the book "we all have stories to tell; it's what makes us human." Zerelda spied his book on display at the local bookstore, and she'd hurried in for a copy. She found herself in many of the entries, but those stories also made her remember some of the more dangerous moments and unsavory characters. At the end of the book, she hoped to read what future writings were in the works but found his obituary instead. He had died a month before the book became available.

The female inmates she knew from those days were now either dead or living far away and unrecognizable from her minds-eye. She'd heard Ada Warnier had been sent to Ionia Insane Asylum and, after hearing nightwatchman Murray had died from blood poisoning, she'd hung herself. The newspaper article had reported the inmate had made braids out of old towels, tied them end to end to fashion a rope, and swung herself from a noose. The irony of how Zerelda's braided bonnets gave beauty and yet Ada's braided noose supplied death was not lost. Seemed as befitting as what she'd heard years ago of a prisoner biting off a guard's thumb and of them both dying within a week of each other from syphilis.

Beyond that, she knew only of Wondrous and so hoped her old friend attended the party. They'd bumped into each other, one coming out while the other one entered the latest new store in the downtown area with women's fashions found more in New York than the Midwest. In an instant, they were those two inmates ready to help each other, ready to tell their life stories, and still be friends. Wondrous had spent ten more years behind those bars, and Zerelda nearly passed her right by at first, not recognizing the woman she'd become. Her friend had glasses on, but her eyes were as clear and sparkling as a burbling stream.

"I can see you," Wondrous had whispered in Zerelda's ear as they hugged.

With arms still wrapped around each other, they

pulled back just far enough to scrutinize their faces for signs of aging. While still in prison, Wondrous had been part of a pro bono program for interns and physicians to help inmates with health problems. She'd had cataract surgery to remove the clouds she'd tried so hard to look through for too many years. To say the least, her life changed with that surgery. While still incarcerated, she began reading—medical books in particular—and soon became part of the team helping other inmates. After thirteen years in Jackson State Prison, she now held the coveted position of head nurse at the largest hospital in the Lansing area. The diamond ring Wondrous thought waited for her at the end of the prison time never came up in any of their conversations. Zerelda didn't feel the need to know as everyone, including herself, feels the need to keep a secret or two hidden away from the rest of the world.

Always in Zerelda's thoughts, her grandma sat with the patience of Job, waiting. Soon the day would come they'd be together again, singing and laughing without a care in the world.

The clock chimed, announcing the witching hour to head downstairs to whoever had shown up. She finished applying a touch of lipstick and fluffed her bobbed hair a bit. No need for a hat tonight. She stood up from the vanity, and a small key dangling from the leather strap caught her eye. She reached down and let the cold metal of the key warm in her hand. Zerelda walked over to the armoire, opened the double doors, and inserted the key into the fourth of twenty drawers in the center of the cabinet. The perfect place for jewelry and other trinkets. There before her were three items—a straight razor, a rugged spike, and a small crystal decanter. She ran her forefinger along the razor's edge, smiling at the memory of Ella's concern of being forgiven all these years later for hiding the blade. In all her innocence, Ella never truly understood how Zerelda had been given this precious gift by hiding real evidence. Because of Ella, many of the lost moments from that horrific night soon fell into place, and as there was nothing more than circumstantial evidence—nothing solid—the conviction had been overturned. Next, Zerelda looked but didn't touch the now-rusty nail. It had come to life in a defining moment of survival, and for that, she'd forever be grateful. Last of all, she slowly removed the topper from the crystal decanter. A slight sour smell drifted upward. Her eyes lost focus.

"Well, Louie, my dear, you gave me a bountiful life, but somehow I could never fully forgive you. You *played the odds* with my life during that trial. I *played the odds* you'd survive an occasional bit of strychnine in your evening meal."